My Secret Unicorn

The Magic Spell
and
Dreams Come True

Two exciting adventures in the
My Secret Unicorn series
together in one bumper book!

★

Have you ever longed for a pony?
Lauren Foster has. When her family moves
to the country, her wish finally comes true.
And Lauren's pony turns out to be even more
special than she had ever dreamed.

Other books in the My Secret Unicorn *series*

FLYING HIGH
STARLIGHT SURPRISE
STRONGER THAN MAGIC
A SPECIAL FRIEND

My Secret Unicorn

The Magic Spell
and
Dreams Come True

Linda Chapman

Illustrated by Biz Hull

PUFFIN

PUFFIN BOOKS

Published by the Penguin Group
Penguin Books Ltd, 80 Strand, London WC2R ORL, England
Penguin Group (USA), Inc., 375 Hudson Street, New York, New York 10014, USA
Penguin Books Australia Ltd, 250 Camberwell Road, Camberwell, Victoria 3124, Australia
Penguin Books Canada Ltd, 10 Alcorn Avenue, Toronto, Ontario, Canada M4V 3B2
Penguin Books India (P) Ltd, 11 Community Centre, Panchsheel Park, New Delhi – 110 017, India
Penguin Books (NZ) Ltd, Cnr Rosedale and Airborne Roads, Albany, Auckland, New Zealand
Penguin Books (South Africa) (Pty) Ltd, 24 Sturdee Avenue, Rosebank 2196, South Africa

Penguin Books Ltd, Registered Offices: 80 Strand, London WC2R ORL, England

www.penguin.com

My Secret Unicorn: The Magic Spell first published 2002
My Secret Unicorn: Dreams Come True first published 2002
First published in one volume 2004

10

Set in 14.25/21.5pt Bembo

Made and printed in England by Clays Ltd, St Ives plc

British Library Cataloguing in Publication Data
A CIP catalogue record for this book is available from the British Library

ISBN 0-141-31838-4

www.greenpenguin.co.uk

Penguin Books is committed to a sustainable future for our business, our readers and our planet. The book in your hands is made from paper certified by the Forest Stewardship Council.

My Secret Unicorn

The Magic Spell

Laura tried to imagine her pony. What colour would he be? How old? Maybe he would be a black pony with four white socks, or a flashy chestnut, or a snow-white pony with a flowing mane and tail. Lauren smiled to herself. Yes, that's what she'd like – a beautiful white pony.

To Peter, for believing in dragons –

and in unicorns

Prologue

Deep in the mountains, mist swirled over a round stone table. A unicorn was standing beside it. With a snort, it lowered its noble head and touched the table's surface with its golden horn.

The table seemed to shiver for a moment. And then its surface began to shine like a mirror.

The unicorn murmured a name.

There was a flash of purple light and the mist cleared.

In the mirror, an image appeared. It was of a small grey pony.

Another unicorn came up to the table. It gazed at the grey pony thoughtfully. 'So, he is still looking for the right owner, to free his powers?' it said.

The golden-horned unicorn nodded its head. 'His last owner was often unkind.'

The other unicorn tossed its mane. Its silvery horn flashed in the light cast by the mirror. 'Surely, somewhere out there there must be someone who is good-hearted enough? Someone who has the imagination to believe in magic?'

'I think there is,' the golden-horned unicorn said softly. 'Watch. She is coming.'

CHAPTER

One

'Where do you want this box, Mum?' Lauren Foster asked, staggering into the kitchen.

Her mum was kneeling on the floor, surrounded by packing cases. 'Just put it anywhere you can find a space, honey,' she said.

Lauren went over to the kitchen table and put the box on it. Just then, Max, her younger brother, came running in. Hot on his heels was Buddy, their ten-week-old Bernese mountain dog.

The puppy came bounding across the floor to say hello – and crashed straight into a stack of crockery that Mrs Foster had just unpacked. A couple of plates fell off the pile with a horrible clatter.

'Oh, Buddy . . .' Mrs Foster sighed.

'It's not his fault,' Max said. He rushed over to scoop the fluffy black and tan puppy into his arms. 'He just hasn't got the hang of stopping yet.'

Mrs Foster laughed. 'Why don't you take Buddy out into the yard?' she suggested. 'You can teach him how to use his brakes.'

Max and Buddy rushed out again into the April afternoon sunshine.

'Watch out, Max!' Mr Foster called from the hallway.

Lauren looked over and saw that Max and Buddy had almost tripped up two removal men on their way out.

Mr Foster, Lauren's dad, was directing the men, who were carrying furniture in from the removal lorry.

'What shall I do now, Dad?' Lauren asked.

'Coming through!' another removal man shouted, drowning out her dad's reply.

Lauren dodged out of the way as the man marched past, carrying the family computer. Mr Foster pushed a hand through his curly brown hair. 'Perhaps it would be best if you went and unpacked your bedroom, honey?' Without giving her a chance to reply, he hurried after the man with the computer. 'Please be careful! That's a delicate piece of equipment!'

Lauren grinned. It was a good idea to escape to her room!

It was strange to think that this house – Granger's Farm – was now her home. As she walked upstairs, Lauren thought about her two best friends back in the city, Carly and Anna. What would they be doing now? Maybe they'd be playing horses or eating the home-made pizzas that Anna's mum often made. Lauren wondered if they were missing her.

Feeling a little lonely, she walked along the landing to the bedroom at the far end and pushed open the white-painted wooden door. Her new room was small with a sloping ceiling. Sunlight streamed into the room through a little window.

Lauren stepped over the piles of boxes and suitcases and sat down on the window-seat to gaze at the view. The towering Blue Ridge Mountains in the distance were majestic and beautiful, but her eyes passed over them and fell on something much nearer to home: the little paddock and stable behind the house.

As she looked at them, her loneliness lifted. She might not know anyone here

in the country but at least she was going to get a pony! A chance to have their own animals had been the first thing her parents had promised when they'd told her and Max about moving from the city.

Mr Foster had decided to follow his dream of becoming a farmer. Max had chosen to have a puppy. They'd got Buddy a couple of weeks ago, and he was already a big part of the family. Everyone loved him. But for as long as Lauren could remember, she had wanted a pony of her own. And her mum was taking her to a horse and pony sale the very next day!

Lauren tried to imagine her pony. What colour would he be? How big? How old? Maybe he would be a black pony with four white socks, or a flashy chestnut or a snow-white pony with a flowing mane and tail. Lauren smiled to herself. Yes, that's what she'd like – a beautiful white pony.

'Lauren!'

Lauren's eyes shot open. It was her mum, calling from the landing. Lauren went to the door.

'I've unpacked some cookies,' her mum said. 'Why don't you come and have some with Max?'

'OK,' Lauren replied. And she went back down to join her family.

By the time Lauren went to bed that night, her bedroom was beginning to look more as if it belonged to her. Her clothes were hanging up in the closet and she had unpacked her books and cuddly toys.

Mrs Foster gently smoothed Lauren's hair. 'Time to get some sleep.'

Suddenly, Lauren didn't want to be left

alone. This was the first night in their new home and it felt a bit strange. 'Will you read me a story, Mum?' she asked. Now that she was nine she didn't usually have a bedtime story. But this was an unusual night.

Her mum seemed to understand. 'Of course, honey,' she said. 'Which one do you want?' She looked at the bookshelf.

'*The Little Pony*,' Lauren said, snuggling down beneath the duvet. *The Little Pony* was her favourite story. Mrs Foster was a writer and she'd written the story especially for Lauren when Lauren was just three years old. It was about a little white pony who travelled the world trying to find a home. He had almost given up when, one day, he met a girl who became his friend. And from then on, they'd looked after each other.

Her mum sat down on the bed and opened the book. As always, she started at the very first page. 'To Lauren, my very own little girl,' she read out softly. And then she started the story. 'Once upon a time, there was a little white pony who wanted a home . . .'

Lauren shut her eyes and smiled at the familiar, comforting words of the story. Halfway between wakefulness and sleep, plans for the next day went round in her head. They were going to a horse and pony sale! *This time tomorrow*, she thought, *I'll have a pony of my own.*

CHAPTER Two

Soon after breakfast, Lauren set off with her mother for the sale. They left Max and her father at home with Buddy.

Even though it was raining, the parking area was already very busy when they arrived. Horses were being led about and the air was filled with shouts and whinnies. Loose dogs darted in between people's legs. Stable-hands dashed around with grooming brushes and saddles.

Lauren felt very excited. 'Where do we go?' she asked.

Her mum pointed out a sign that said LIVESTOCK. 'The horses and ponies will be over there. The bidding should have just started.'

Lauren followed her mum through the crowds until they came to a large covered ring.

A bay horse was being trotted around the ring by a stable-hand. A man standing on a platform at one end was calling out a price, raising his voice above the noise of the rain drumming on the roof. 'One thousand, two hundred dollars I'm bid.

Do I have any advance on one thousand, two hundred?'

A woman near Lauren held up her hand.

The man nodded at her. 'One thousand, three hundred to the lady on my left. Any advance on one thousand, three hundred dollars?'

Lauren turned to her mum. 'So the person who offers the most money gets the horse?'

Her mum nodded. 'The auctioneer – that's the man on the platform – keeps raising the price until no one else bids.'

'Any advance on one thousand, three hundred?' the auctioneer shouted. No one moved. He raised a small wooden hammer. 'Going, going – gone!' he said, bringing the hammer down on the table beside him with a bang. 'Sold to the lady on my left.'

The lady smiled and the horse was led out of the ring. A new horse – a big dapple-grey – was brought in by another stable-hand.

'Come on, let's go and look around,' Mrs Foster said to Lauren. She led the way towards an enormous barn beside the ring. Lauren gasped when she looked inside. It was full of pens and nearly all had horses standing in them. There were bays and chestnuts and greys, each awaiting their turn in the ring. Lauren thought they all looked very big.

Lauren's mother had disappeared ahead

of her through a gate, but Lauren didn't want to walk too quickly; she didn't want to miss a thing. Carefully she picked her way through the puddles underfoot and made her way through the crowd. She reached the gate at the same time as an elderly lady who was sheltering beneath a brightly coloured umbrella. Lauren held the gate open for her.

The lady nodded. 'Thank you,' she said.

Lauren followed her through. The lady suddenly slipped on the wet ground and almost fell. 'Careful!' Lauren cried. She reached forward to hold the lady's elbow until she had regained her balance.

'Thank you again,' the lady said, her face creasing into a wide smile. She had

the friendliest blue eyes that Lauren had ever seen.

'You're welcome,' Lauren said, smiling. 'I'm Lauren,' she went on.

'Hello, Lauren,' the lady answered. 'So if you're here at the sale, I guess you like ponies.'

Lauren nodded. 'I love them! My parents are going to buy me one.' She didn't want to sound spoilt, but she couldn't stop herself from blurting out her amazing news.

'Aren't you lucky?' The lady's eyes twinkled as they met Lauren's.

'I'm the luckiest person in the world,' Lauren breathed. 'Will you be OK now? I ought to get going. My mother will be wondering where I am.'

'I'll be just fine, thank you,' the lady replied. 'I hope you find the pony you're looking for.'

'Thank you,' Lauren said. She scanned the crowds anxiously for her mother. Spotting her, she looked back to say goodbye to the old lady, but she had already slipped away.

Lauren shrugged and quickly made her way into the barn, past the horses. As she rounded the corner, she saw her mum ahead of her, at the end of the barn. She was standing beside a row of about ten ponies. Lauren ran to her.

'There you are, Lauren!' her mother exclaimed. 'I thought I'd lost you.'

'Not a chance,' Lauren grinned. She looked excitedly at the ponies in front of her.

In the first pen, there was a tiny black pony. The next pen was empty, but beside it there were two pretty chestnuts with matching white stars. Next to them was an old grey mare with feathery legs and a large head, and beside her was a cheeky-looking bay. On the door of each pen there was a card with details about the pony inside.

There was no sparkling white pony like Lauren had been imagining, but she didn't care. 'They're all lovely!' she gasped, turning around to her mum.

'Well, this one's much too small,' Mrs Foster said, as she looked at the little black pony. 'We want a pony who's about thirteen hands high and at least six years old. Any younger and he'll be too inexperienced.'

Lauren ran over to the bay gelding's pen and looked at the card attached to his gate. 'Topper,' she read out. 'Thirteen hands. Four years old.' She felt a flicker of disappointment. He was too young. She patted him and moved on.

The grey mare was too tall, the black pony was too small, and the chestnut ponies were only three years old. Lauren walked along the line of ponies, reading their sale notices. She reached the end of the row. Not one of them was right.

Her mum came up behind her and squeezed her shoulder. 'Maybe we won't find your perfect pony today. We can always come to the next sale. It's only a month away.'

A month! Lauren looked around. She couldn't wait that long. 'The little black pony isn't that small,' she began desperately. 'And he's really cute . . .'

Just then, she heard the sound of hooves. She swung around. A man was leading a scruffy grey pony out of the vet's tent and down the walkway towards the last empty pen. 'I thought I wasn't going to get here in time for the sale,' he said, noticing Lauren and her mum.

The pony looked quiet and sad.

'Hi, boy,' Lauren said, going over to him.

At the sound of her voice, the pony lifted his head and pricked his ears. He whinnied and Lauren felt her heart flip. Suddenly she didn't care that he was scruffy and dirty. This was the pony she wanted. 'How old is he?' she asked the pony's owner.

'Twilight? He's seven,' the man replied.

Lauren swung around to her mum. 'He's the right age!' The pony stepped forward and thrust his nose into her hands. His breath was warm as he nuzzled at her fingers.

'Can we buy him?' Lauren asked her mother eagerly.

The man smiled at them. 'Are you looking for a pony?'

'Yes, we are,' Mrs Foster replied. She walked forward and looked at Twilight. 'Why's he for sale, Mr –?'

'Roberts – Cliff Roberts,' the man said, introducing himself and shaking hands.

'The pony's for sale because my daughter, Jade, doesn't want him any more,' he explained. 'I only bought Twilight for her a few months ago but she says he's too quiet and not showy enough. I've just bought her a new pony to take to shows, so now I've got to sell Twilight.'

'Can we buy him?' Lauren asked her mum again.

'Well, you'll have to have a ride on him first,' her mum said. She turned to Twilight's owner. 'Would that be possible, Mr Roberts?'

Mr Roberts smiled. 'Of course. It looks like the rain has stopped now. I'll just go and get the saddle.'

★

Five minutes later, Lauren found herself riding Twilight around the exercise paddock. He felt wonderful. The slightest squeeze of her legs made him go faster and the smallest pull on the reins slowed him down. It was almost as though he could read her mind.

'That's amazing!' Mr Roberts said, as Lauren brought Twilight to a halt by the paddock gate and dismounted. 'He hardly wanted to do anything for Jade. He must like you.'

'I love him!' Lauren said, her eyes shining. She stretched out her hands towards Twilight. The pony lowered his muzzle and blew softly on Lauren's face. 'Please can we buy him?' she begged her

mother. 'He's perfect!'

'He certainly seems very well behaved,' Mrs Foster said, patting Twilight. 'Maybe we'll bid for him when he goes into the ring.'

Lauren thought about the sale and the way the person who offered the most money got the pony. 'But someone else might bid more than us,' she said in alarm. 'Can't we just buy him now?'

'I'm quite happy to arrange a private sale, if you're interested,' Mr Roberts said to Lauren's mother. 'I wouldn't have to pay the auction fee then, so it would save me some money. How about we say . . .' He thought for a moment and then named a price. 'I'll even throw in the saddle and bridle if you like.'

Lauren looked at her mum and crossed her fingers. She didn't think she could bear to see Twilight go into the ring and be sold to someone else. *Oh, please*, she prayed. *Please say yes.*

To her amazement, her mum smiled. 'OK, Mr Roberts. You've got yourself a deal.'

Lauren could hardly believe it. She threw her arms round Twilight's neck and hugged him. 'Oh, Twilight!' she gasped in delight. 'You're going to be mine!'

The little grey pony nuzzled her happily, as if he understood.

CHAPTER

Three

It was soon arranged that Mr Roberts would drive Twilight round to Granger's Farm the next morning.

'That gives us time to buy everything we need and get the paddock and stable ready,' Mrs Foster said to Lauren.

On the way home Lauren and her mum drove to the local tack store on the outskirts of the town.

The sales assistant, a girl called Jenny, was very helpful. Soon there were loads of horsy things on the counter – brushes, a first-aid kit, feed buckets, a head-collar. The pile grew bigger and bigger until, at last, Lauren had everything she needed.

Jenny helped them pack all their purchases into their car. 'Have fun with your new pony!' she called to Lauren.

Lauren grinned at her. 'Thanks! I will!'

As Jenny went back to the store, Lauren noticed a small bookshop tucked between the tack store and a shop selling electrical goods. It had an old-fashioned brown and gold sign over the window saying MRS FONTANA'S NEW AND USED BOOKS. 'Look at that bookshop, Mum,' she said.

'Shall we take a look inside?' Mrs Foster asked.

Lauren nodded eagerly. Both she and her mum loved bookshops, and this one looked really interesting.

They walked along the pavement. Through the glass panel in the door, Lauren could see a cheerful rose-patterned carpet, and shelves and shelves of books.

Mrs Foster pushed the door open. A bell tinkled and they stepped inside.

'Wow!' Lauren said, looking around. There were books everywhere! Old books, new books – and not just on the shelves. There were piles of books next to the shelves. And more piles in front of those! But enough space had been left for a few chairs to be placed round a pretty iron fireplace. A large notice said: *Please feel free to browse and sit awhile*. It was the strangest, loveliest bookshop that Lauren had ever been in.

Just then there was a pattering of feet, and a little white terrier dog with a black patch over one eye came trotting up to them. 'Look, Mum!' Lauren exclaimed. She crouched down and the terrier licked her hand.

Mrs Foster bent down to stroke him. 'Hi, little one,' she said.

'Isn't he cute?' said Lauren.

'Ah, I see you've met Walter.'

Lauren and her mum looked up. An elderly lady was coming towards them. She was wearing an embroidered shawl over a flowery dress. Lauren gasped. It was the lady she'd met at the horse sale earlier! There was no mistaking the warm blue eyes.

'Hello, Lauren,' the lady said, smiling.

'You two know each other?' Lauren's mother said, looking surprised.

'We met at the horse and pony sale this morning,' the lady explained. She held out her hand. 'I'm Mrs Fontana,' she said. 'This is my shop.'

'Alice Foster,' Lauren's mum said, shaking hands. 'We've just moved into the area. Is it OK if we have a look around?'

'Feel free,' Mrs Fontana replied. She smiled at Lauren. 'There are lots of books in the side room you might like.'

Leaving her mum to browse, Lauren made her way to the side of the shop. The next room was full of children's books. There were no bright posters or colourful displays like there were in most bookshops, but there were lots of plump, soft cushions on the floor and a big table piled high with all kinds of books.

Lauren examined each pile and quickly picked out a collection of pony stories. She sat down on one of the cushions and started to read.

Suddenly she heard the patter of paws coming towards her. It was Walter, the

terrier. He sat down beside Lauren and looked at her, his head cocked on one side. Lauren tickled him under the chin.

'He likes you,' Mrs Fontana said.

Lauren jumped. The old lady seemed to

have appeared out of nowhere.

She smiled again at Lauren. 'So what have you chosen, my dear?'

Feeling slightly shy, Lauren showed Mrs Fontana the book of pony stories.

'I thought you might like those,' Mrs Fontana said, raising her bright eyes to Lauren's face. 'Did you find your pony today?'

'I certainly did,' Lauren said, nodding excitedly. 'He's coming tomorrow. He's called Twilight and he's wonderful!'

Mrs Fontana stared at her for a moment and then she swung around. 'You know what?' she said. 'I think I might have just the thing for you. It's up here.'

Lauren watched as Mrs Fontana fetched a folding stepladder and stood on it to reach the top shelf. 'Here we are,' the old lady said, pulling out a dusty purple book. She climbed down the ladder and handed the book to Lauren.

Lauren looked down at the heavy leather volume. It had beautiful gold writing on the cover. Lauren looked at the words. '*The Life of a Unicorn*,' she read out.

She opened the book. The pages were smooth and yellow with age. There was lots of writing, but also some beautiful pictures. Unicorns cantered in the sky and grazed on soft grass. 'They're lovely,' she said as she turned the pages.

'Yes,' Mrs Fontana agreed, sighing.

Lauren stopped at the next picture. There was no unicorn to be seen, just a small grey pony.

'That's a young unicorn,' Mrs Fontana said, looking over her shoulder.

'But it hasn't got a horn,' Lauren said.

'Ah, but, you see, young unicorns don't have horns,' Mrs Fontana told her. 'They only grow their horns and receive their magical powers when they hear some magic words on their second birthday. Then they turn into the creatures that we know as unicorns.'

Lauren looked at her in surprise. From the way Mrs Fontana was talking, she made it sound as if unicorns were real.

'But unicorns don't really exist, do they?' Lauren said to the old lady. 'They're just made up, like fairies and dragons and trolls.'

'You don't think fairies, dragons and trolls exist either?' Mrs Fontana said, raising her eyebrows.

'No way,' Lauren grinned.

'Why not?' Mrs Fontana said.

Looking into Mrs Fontana's blue eyes, Lauren suddenly felt less certain. 'Well, no one has ever seen them,' she faltered.

'Maybe that's because they don't *want* to be seen,' Mrs Fontana said. She looked around and then leaned forward. 'Shall I tell you a secret? I've seen a unicorn.'

Lauren stared at her in astonishment. Had Mrs Fontana gone crazy?

Mrs Fontana seemed to read her mind. 'Oh, I'm not mad, dear,' she said with a smile. 'All it needs are the magic words, spoken by the right person, a handful of the secret flowers – and a unicorn, of course.'

Just then there was the sound of footsteps. 'Are you ready, honey?' Mrs Foster asked. 'We should be going home.'

Mrs Fontana stood up briskly. Lauren felt as if she had been jerked out of a dream.

'What's that?' her mum said, seeing the book in Lauren's hands.

'A . . . a book on unicorns,' Lauren said, standing up.

Mrs Foster glanced at the book. She

took in the soft leather binding and the pictures, glowing in jewel colours. 'It looks very expensive, honey. I'm afraid we can't afford it,' she said.

Lauren nodded. She hadn't really expected her mum to buy it for her.

'I'd like you to have it,' Mrs Fontana said softly.

Lauren looked at her in amazement.

The old lady smiled. 'Think of it as a gift to welcome you to the town.'

'But, Mrs Fontana, that's much too generous . . .' Mrs Foster began.

'Not at all,' said Mrs Fontana. 'It's a very special book and it needs a good home. Something tells me that Lauren will look after it.'

'Oh, I will!' Lauren gasped. 'Thank you, Mrs Fontana.' She took the book in her hands and held it close to her.

The bookshop owner showed them to the door. 'Do call again,' she said. 'And good luck at Granger's Farm.'

'We will – and thank you so much for the welcome gift,' Mrs Foster said.

The door tinkled shut behind them. Lauren was suddenly struck by a thought. 'How did Mrs Fontana know that we had moved to Granger's Farm? We didn't tell her.'

Mrs Foster frowned. 'Didn't we?'

'No,' Lauren said.

Her mum shrugged. 'Oh, well, it's a small town. News has probably got around. Now, come on. Dad and Max will be wondering where we are.'

They got into the car. As her mum started the engine, Lauren looked back once more at the bookshop. Walter, the little dog, was sitting in the window, staring out. It looked just as if he was smiling at them.

CHAPTER

Four

As Mrs Foster drove back to Granger's Farm, Lauren looked at the beautiful book she had been given. When she came to the page with the picture of the baby unicorn, she could almost hear Mrs Fontana's voice saying, *I've seen a unicorn*.

Lauren gently stroked the picture with her fingertip. She was sure that Mrs

Fontana must have been making up all that stuff about magical creatures. The old lady couldn't really have seen a unicorn.

Could she?

Of course she couldn't, Lauren told herself firmly. *Unicorns don't exist. Mrs Fontana has just been reading one too many of her old books.*

'So, what have you bought?' Mr Foster asked, coming out to meet them as they pulled up at the farm. Max ran out after him.

'Lots,' Lauren said, jumping out of the car.

'Can I see?' said Max, opening the back door. He pulled a hoof pick out of one of the bags. 'What's this for?'

'Come on, Max,' Mr Foster said. 'Lauren can explain while we unload.'

They carried the bags to the stable, and then Mrs Foster went into the house to do some more unpacking while Lauren, her dad and Max carried the purchases for Twilight into the little shed which was going to be his tack room. Mr Foster hammered two metal hooks into the wall, one for Twilight's bridle and one for his new red and blue head-collar. Then he fetched a low table and an old striped rug from the garage.

With the rug on the floor, a light bulb gleaming brightly and Lauren's shiny new grooming kit and first-aid box laid out

on the table, the tack room looked very cosy and cheerful.

'This is great,' Lauren said, looking around happily.

'Now all we need is Twilight,' Mr Foster said, smiling at Lauren.

Lauren imagined Twilight's grey head looking out over the stable door. 'I can't wait till tomorrow!' she said.

That night, when Lauren went to bed, she opened the book that Mrs Fontana had given her and began to read the first chapter. '*Noah and the unicorns*,' she whispered quietly to herself . . .

Many years ago, there was a great flood that threatened both animals and magical creatures. The magical creatures fled to safety in Arcadia, an enchanted land that can't be found by humans.

Meanwhile, a man called Noah gathered together two of every animal and took them on to the Ark he had built. As the rain started to fall, Noah saw two small grey ponies in the grassy meadows beside the rising sea. He took them on to his Ark with the rest of the animals.

Through a magic mirror, the unicorns in Arcadia watched gratefully as Noah took care of their young. For these two grey ponies were, in fact, baby unicorns who hadn't yet grown into their magical powers. They had been left behind in the rush to Arcadia.

Whilst on the Ark, the time for the two young unicorns to gain their magical powers came and went. They had lost their chance. And the unicorns in Arcadia mourned.

When a whole year had passed, the floods went down. Noah released the young unicorns on to the Earth with the other animals. And there they remained, trapped in their pony bodies.

Back in Arcadia, the watching unicorns worked on a Turning Spell that would give the unicorns another chance to gain their magical powers. The spell took years and years to perfect. At last it was ready. But the spell would only free a unicorn if spoken by a good-hearted human who believed in magic.

A very brave unicorn risked his own powers to fly back to Earth. He searched long and hard for a human to whom he could entrust the spell. Eventually he found her.

The spell worked – and the two young

unicorns became great friends with the human who had helped them. They grew beautiful horns and flew like angels. And together they had many magical adventures . . .

CHAPTER

Five

Lauren put the book down. The way the book was written made everything about unicorns sound so real, not like a made-up story at all. She looked at the picture at the end of the chapter. It showed a beautiful unicorn cantering up into the sky.

I wish the story was true, Lauren thought. *I wish there were still unicorns on the Earth.*

I'd love to help one.

And then she smiled. Unicorns might not exist, but Twilight did and he was going to arrive the very next day.

Mr Roberts arrived with Twilight at ten o'clock. He opened the side door of the trailer so that Lauren could get inside. Twilight whinnied as she stepped into the trailer.

'Hello, little one,' Lauren said, stroking his nose.

Twilight looked at her. *Hello*, his dark eyes seemed to say back.

Mr Roberts lowered the ramp to the ground. 'You can bring him out now, Lauren!' he called.

Lauren untied Twilight and backed carefully out of the trailer. Her mum and dad and Max came over.

'Hello, boy,' Mrs Foster said, feeding Twilight a carrot.

'He's really dirty, isn't he?' Max said, as he patted Twilight and a cloud of dust flew into the air.

Twilight whinnied indignantly, as if he understood what Max had said.

Mr Roberts smiled ruefully. 'I'm afraid my daughter has been busy with her new pony. She hasn't been looking after Twilight as well as she might.' He looked at Lauren. 'You'd like Jade. She's just crazy about ponies.'

Lauren wasn't so sure. If Mr Roberts's

daughter was really crazy about ponies, she would have looked after Twilight better. But she didn't say anything.

While Mr and Mrs Foster sorted out paying Mr Roberts, Lauren and Max led Twilight to his stable.

'Are you going to ride now, Lauren?' Max asked.

'I'm going to groom him first,' Lauren replied.

She tied Twilight up outside the stable and fetched the grooming kit.

'Can I help?' asked Max.

'OK,' Lauren said, handing him a brush with thick bristles called a dandy brush. It was good for getting rid of dirt and dust. 'You can brush him with that.'

Twilight nuzzled her shoulder. Lauren smiled happily and kissed his face. She didn't think she'd ever felt happier in her life.

Two hours later, Twilight was looking much smarter. Lauren and Max had brushed him and washed his mane and tail. Instead of being a dirty grey colour, he was now pale grey. The dust had come out of his coat and Lauren had replaced the old, tatty head-collar he had been wearing with the new red and blue one that she and her mum had bought the day before. However, despite everything, Twilight still looked a bit scruffy. His coat didn't really shine, and the long hair

around his hooves and under his chin was quite straggly. Still, Lauren didn't mind.

With her mum's help, Lauren tacked

Twilight up and rode him into the paddock. Just like the day before, he seemed to know exactly what she wanted him to do, and soon they were cantering around the field. When Lauren finally stopped him by the gate, her face was flushed and her eyes were shining. 'He's just great!' she said to her mum, who was watching with Max. 'Can I go for a ride in the woods?' She saw her mum look doubtful. 'I won't go far.'

'OK,' Mrs Foster agreed. 'But don't stay out too long.'

'I won't. I promise,' Lauren said. She remounted and rode Twilight out of the paddock. The mountain that rose up behind the farmhouse was thickly wooded and, as she rode Twilight into the trees, she felt his ears prick and his step quicken.

Lauren smiled happily. 'You like it up here, don't you, boy?'

Twilight snorted and broke into a trot.

Lauren let him have his head and he broke into a canter. They made their way along the trail. The air was quiet so that the only sound, apart from the thudding of Twilight's hooves on the soft ground, was the distant calling of birds in the tops of the trees. Lauren felt that she could have gone on forever. But she remembered what she had promised her mum, so she slowed Twilight down to turn him around.

Twilight looked to one side. A small

side-trail led off the main track. He pulled towards it. Lauren stopped him. 'No,' she told him. 'We've got to go back now.' Twilight pulled towards the side-trail again.

'We'll go another day,' Lauren told him and then, turning him around, she rode back to the farm.

That night, when Lauren went to bed, she opened the unicorn book to a beautiful picture showing unicorns grazing in lush meadows dotted with star-shaped purple flowers. The pink sky was streaked across with orange and gold, as if the sun was setting. She began to read . . .

When the two young unicorns grew old they returned to Arcadia. The unicorn elders decided that from then on they would send young unicorns to Earth to do good works. They look like small ponies. Each of them hopes to find someone who will learn how to free their magical powers. To do this one needs: the words of the Turning Spell, a hair from the unicorn's mane, the petals from a single moonflower and the light of the Twilight Star, which only shines for ten minutes after the sun has set.

Lauren turned the page and saw the picture of the young unicorn that she had seen in Mrs Fontana's shop. Scruffy and grey, it looked quite like Twilight.

Maybe Twilight's a unicorn in disguise, Lauren thought suddenly.

She smiled to herself. She was being silly. It was just a made-up story and Twilight was just a regular pony.

CHAPTER Six

After breakfast the next morning, Lauren took Twilight out for a ride in the woods again. It felt a bit lonely on her own. *I wish I had someone else to ride with*, she thought. She wondered if she would make friends with someone when school started.

As they reached the trees, Twilight pricked up his ears and pulled at the reins.

'OK, boy,' Lauren said, letting him trot.

She had been riding for ten minutes when Twilight suddenly stopped.

'Go on!' Lauren encouraged him.

But Twilight wouldn't move. He shook his head and looked to the left.

Lauren realized that he was looking along the same side-trail he had tried to go down the last time they had been in the woods. She thought for a moment. What harm could there be in exploring?

'All right,' she said, turning Twilight towards it.

The track was narrow and the trees on either side met over Lauren's head, blocking out the sun. It was like riding through a long, green tunnel. As the silence closed in around them, Lauren began to wonder where the track was leading.

'Maybe we should turn back,' she whispered to Twilight, but the pony pulled eagerly on the reins. It was clear he didn't want to stop.

Lauren saw light ahead. It looked as if the track was coming to an end. Wondering where they would come out, she let Twilight carry on. He trotted out from among the trees and into a grassy glade.

It was beautiful. In the centre of the glade there was a mound dotted with purple flowers where a cloud of yellow butterflies fluttered in the sunlight.

Twilight walked to the mound and Lauren saw that the flowers were star-shaped and at the tip of each bright petal

there was a golden spot. She frowned. She knew she had seen them somewhere before, but she couldn't remember where.

With a soft whicker, Twilight bent his head. Thinking he was grabbing a mouthful of grass, Lauren tried to pull his head up. 'No, Twilight!'

But as she spoke she realized that he wasn't eating, he was nuzzling at the star-shaped flowers. Her curiosity was aroused and she dismounted.

Looping the reins round her arm, she looked closely at the flowers. Where *had* she seen them before?

Twilight whickered and nudged her arm. Lauren was puzzled. It was as if he was trying to tell her something, she thought, then she shook her head.

He's just a pony, she reminded herself quickly.

She glanced around. The glade was so beautiful and still that she didn't want to leave. But she knew that she ought to be getting home, so she mounted Twilight and rode him back into the trees.

Lauren turned Twilight on to the main trail through the woods where the birds were singing overhead again. Leaning forward, she let him go faster and they cantered along the track towards home.

When they got back to the farm, Lauren went into the study, where her dad had loads of books about plants. She took the biggest one down from the shelf and began to look through the section on woodland flowers. There were quite a few plants with purple flowers but none of them was star-shaped with golden spots on the edge of the petals. She tried another book and then another. But she couldn't find any flowers that looked like the ones in the glade.

She closed the last book and sighed. She knew she had seen the flowers before somewhere.

'I thought I heard you in here,' Mrs Foster said, coming into the study. 'What are you doing?'

'I've been trying to find the name of some flowers I saw in the woods,' Lauren replied. She wondered if her mum would know what they were. 'They were purple, sort of star-shaped with a gold spot at the tip of each petal.'

'Sorry, I can't help you,' her mum said. 'They sound very unusual, though. Now,' she went on, changing the subject, 'we need to get you some things for school – you start next week. Why don't you run upstairs and get changed and we'll go to the mall?'

'OK,' Lauren said.

She hurried up to her room and pulled on a pair of clean jeans and a sweatshirt. The unicorn book was lying on her bedside table. It was still open at the picture of the unicorns grazing. As Lauren did up her jeans, she glanced at it again: the unicorns, the grassy meadows, the purple flowers . . .

The purple flowers!

She stared at the picture. They were exactly the same as the ones she had just seen in the wood!

CHAPTER

Seven

Lauren snatched up the book. The flowers in the picture had the same star shape, the same gold spot. A wild thought filled her mind. The book had said that unicorns disguised as ponies could be changed back by saying a magic spell and using a certain type of flower. What if the flowers she had found in the wood were the very ones that were needed in the spell?

She quickly turned the pages of the book until she found the part that explained how unicorns disguised as ponies could be changed back into unicorns. In the middle of the page there was a small picture of a purple flower just like the ones in the wood. Lauren read the words under the picture.

The moonflower: a rare purple-flowering herb that is used in the Turning Spell.

Lauren stared. She'd found the flower that the book said could give a unicorn its magical powers. She remembered the way Twilight had been nuzzling at the flowers

in the glade. Maybe the story was true . . . and maybe, just maybe, Twilight really was a unicorn in disguise!

Her heart started to race. If she could

just find the words of the spell, then she could try it out.

'Lauren! Are you coming?' her mum called.

Lauren could hardly bear to put the book down. The spell had to be here somewhere.

'Lauren!' her mum called again.

Lauren closed the book reluctantly. 'I'm coming!' she called, and she went downstairs.

Normally Lauren loved buying things for a new school term, but not that day. All she could think about was unicorns.

On the way home, Mrs Foster stopped

by the tack store to pick up a couple of spare feed buckets.

Lauren had an idea. 'Can I go and look in the bookshop?' she asked.

'Sure,' Mrs Foster agreed. 'I'll meet you there in a few minutes.'

Lauren ran to the bookshop. The doorbell tinkled as she went inside. The shop was just as she remembered it: the piles of books, the rose-patterned carpet. She caught sight of the owner near the back of the shop. 'Mrs Fontana!' she called.

The old lady turned around. 'Hello, dear,' she said. 'What can I do for you?'

Suddenly Lauren didn't know what to say. Mrs Fontana looked so calm and ordinary that the whole idea of asking her if she knew what the magic spell was seemed really dumb. 'Um . . . well . . . I . . .' Lauren stammered.

'So, have you seen a unicorn yet?' Mrs Fontana said softly.

Lauren stopped stammering and stared.

'That's what you wanted to come in and talk to me about, isn't it?' Mrs Fontana said.

Lauren didn't even stop to ask how the old lady knew. 'Is the story really true?' she gasped.

Mrs Fontana smiled. 'It's true for those who want it to be true.'

'Do you know what the spell is?' Lauren asked eagerly.

'I do, but I can't tell you,' the old lady replied. 'Those who want to find unicorns must do it for themselves. You have everything you need.'

'But . . .' Lauren began.

Just then Walter gave a warning bark. The shop door swung open and Lauren's mum came in. 'Hello, Mrs Fontana,' she said.

'Hello,' the bookshop owner said with a smile. 'So how are you settling in at Granger's Farm?' Her tone changed and now she sounded brisk and efficient.

Lauren waited while the two adults chatted. She felt frustrated. If Mrs Fontana really knew what the spell was, why wouldn't she tell it to her? She longed to ask the bookshop owner more, but she couldn't with her mum standing there.

Lauren thought about the old lady's words: *You have everything you need.*

What did she mean?

That night, when she went to bed, Lauren decided to read the book from the beginning through to the end.

Starting at the first chapter, she began to read slowly and carefully. She read that after the floods had gone down, the magical creatures decided not to live on Earth any more and stayed in Arcadia. Arcadia was ruled by seven Golden Unicorns who watched the Earth through a magic mirror.

Lauren read on, but she didn't find the spell.

She awoke the following morning to see the book lying beside her on her bed. She had just two chapters left to read. She wondered whether to start on them, but then she saw that it was seven o'clock. It was time to get up and give Twilight his breakfast. She took the book outside with her. She could read it while he was eating.

Leaving it in the tack room, she brought Twilight in from the paddock and put him in his stall. Then she mixed up his feed. The sooner Twilight was fed, the sooner she could read a little more.

Quickly, Lauren emptied the feed into the manger and then she fetched the book. Carrying it into his stable, she sat down on an upturned bucket and began to read. Surely the spell had to be in the book somewhere!

Lauren became aware that Twilight had stopped eating. He was staring at the book. With a snort, he walked over to her.

'Hello, boy,' she said.

Twilight blew gently. The pages of the book fluttered over.

'Twilight! You've lost my place!' Lauren said. But before she could turn back to the page she had been reading, Twilight breathed out again.

'What are you doing?' Lauren asked, as he nuzzled his soft lips against the back cover. They left a damp mark on the paper and she made to push his muzzle away but, as she did so, she realized that the last page of the book had been glued to the back cover. One corner of the page fluttered slightly as Twilight breathed on the book.

Lauren carefully pulled at it. The glue gave way and the page turned.

Inside the cover were some faint words written in pencil. It looked like a poem of some sort. Lauren read the title: *The Turning Spell*.

CHAPTER Eight

Trembling with excitement, Lauren read the faintly pencilled words:

Twilight Star, Twilight Star,
Twinkling high above so far.
Shining light, shining bright,
Will you grant my wish tonight?
Let my little horse forlorn
Be at last a unicorn!

Her eyes flew to Twilight. 'Oh, Twilight,' she whispered. 'It's the spell!'

Twilight bent his head as if he was nodding.

Lauren jumped to her feet. She had to take Twilight to the woods and pick one of those flowers!

After giving Twilight time to digest his breakfast, Lauren tacked him up and rode into the woods. Twilight seemed to know just where they were going. With his ears pricked up he cantered along the track until they came to the little side-trail.

They turned down the narrow track and followed it until they reached the sunny glade. It looked just the same as the day before. A cloud of butterflies swooped over the grass and the air had an expectant feeling.

Lauren dismounted and led Twilight over to the grassy mound, where she found a single purple flower that had fallen to the ground. She picked it up. As she did so, a sharp tingle ran down her spine.

She felt Twilight's warm breath on her shoulder and she looked at him. 'Oh, Twilight,' she whispered. 'I hope this is going to work.'

'Dad, what time does the sun set?' Lauren asked her father that afternoon. Her book had said that the Twilight Star only shone for ten minutes after the sun had set and that the spell had to be performed then.

'About seven o'clock at the moment,' her dad said. 'Why?'

'I just wondered,' Lauren said quickly.

At six-thirty her mum put supper out.

Lauren ate as fast as she could. 'May I leave the table, please?' she asked as soon as her plate was empty.

Her mum looked surprised. 'You know better, Lauren – not till everyone's finished,' she said.

So Lauren had to wait. Through the kitchen window she watched the sun dropping lower and lower in the sky. She was going to miss the sunset!

At long last her dad put his knife and fork down. 'That was delicious,' he said.

Before he had even finished speaking, Lauren had jumped to her feet. 'Can I go and see Twilight now, Mum?' she begged.

'All right,' Mrs Foster said. 'Go on.'

Lauren grabbed her jacket and ran out of the door. The book was still in the tack room. She fetched it and raced down to the paddock. Her heart was pounding in her chest. What would happen? Would the spell really work?

Twilight was standing by the gate. He whinnied when he saw her. Lauren led him towards the far corner of the field. It was shaded by trees and hidden from the house by the stable block.

As soon as they were out of sight of the house, Lauren carefully pulled a single hair out of Twilight's mane, opened the book and took the flower out of her pocket. The gold spots on the petals seemed to glow in the last rays of the sun.

She looked up. The final curve of the sun was just sinking on the horizon. Lauren's eyes narrowed as she searched for the star. But there was nothing. Maybe she had missed it? Twilight whickered.

'Ssh, Twilight,' Lauren said. She turned and patted his neck. Then she looked back up into the sky, and she gasped. High above her, a star had appeared. It was time for the spell!

'Please work,' Lauren whispered. She took a deep, trembling breath and began to tear the petals off the flower. As she did so, she read the spell out.

The Magic Spell

Twilight Star, Twilight Star,
Twinkling high above so far.
Shining light, shining bright,
Will you grant my wish tonight?
Let my little horse forlorn
Be at last a unicorn!

As she read the last word, she held her breath.

Nothing happened.

Lauren looked down at the petals in her hand and felt a wave of disappointment hit her. It was just a story after all.

She looked at Twilight and felt tears prickle in her eyes. She had so badly wanted him to be a unicorn.

Swallowing hard, she dropped the

petals on the ground.

There was a flash of purple light, so bright that it made Lauren shut her eyes. When she opened them again, she gasped.

Twilight had disappeared!

CHAPTER

Nine

Lauren swung around, looking for Twilight. A snow-white unicorn was flying in the sky behind her. Its hooves and horn gleamed silver and its mane and tail swirled around it.

'Twilight?' Lauren gasped.

'Yes,' the unicorn said. 'It's me. It feels a bit wobbly up here. This is the first time I've flown. Whoops . . .' He flew down through the air towards Lauren, narrowly missing a low branch. With a kick of his hind legs, he landed on the grass beside her. 'Hello,' he said, walking over and nuzzling her.

Although Twilight's words rang out clearly in Lauren's head, his mouth didn't move.

'You can talk!' Lauren said in astonishment.

'Only while I'm in my magical shape,' Twilight told her. 'And you'll only be able to hear me if you're touching me or holding a hair from my mane.'

'I can't believe you're really a unicorn!' Lauren exclaimed.

Twilight laughed. 'Well, I am. I was

trapped in my pony body, but you freed me, Lauren, and that means you are my Unicorn Friend.'

'Unicorn Friend?' Lauren echoed.

Twilight nodded his beautiful head. 'Yes. Every unicorn is looking for a Unicorn Friend to do good deeds with.'

'So everything in that book is true?' Lauren gasped.

'Everything,' Twilight replied, merrily tossing his mane. He knelt down by bending his forelegs. 'Climb on my back and let's try flying together. You'll have to excuse me if I'm a bit wobbly.'

Lauren took hold of his mane and mounted. 'What if I fall off?'

'You can't fall while I am in my

magical shape,' Twilight said. 'Unicorn magic will keep you safe.'

Lauren grabbed his mane and he plunged forward into a canter.

'Whoa . . . hold on tight!' Twilight called.

Twilight's hooves skimmed across the grass and the ground dropped away. 'Here we go!' he called to her.

His back legs kicked down powerfully and with a jolt they flew up into the air, lurching from side to side.

'Don't worry, I'll soon get the hang of this,' Twilight said confidently.

Lauren held on tight. 'Wow!' she gasped as she looked down.

Twilight surged upwards towards the

stars and the wind streamed through Lauren's hair as they settled into a steadier pace. 'This is amazing!' she cried.

She looked down. Below her she could see her house and the woods.

Suddenly Lauren caught sight of a figure walking out of the trees. A white terrier dog with a black patch trotted at the person's side. 'It's Mrs Fontana!' she exclaimed.

The old lady looked up and raised her hand in greeting. 'Hello there!' she called.

Twilight swooped towards her and landed lightly on the soft grass.

Lauren scrambled off Twilight's back. 'Mrs Fontana!' she gasped.

Mrs Fontana smiled at Lauren. 'I see

you've found yourself a friend.'

Lauren nodded. 'Thank you for giving me the book!' she said.

'It was time it had a new owner,' Mrs Fontana replied. 'But you must promise to guard the secret carefully. A unicorn's powers can attract bad people who want to use the magic selfishly. You must not

tell a soul. Do you understand?'

At first Lauren felt disappointed. She had been thinking how amazed her mum and dad would be when she told them. But she could see the sense in what Mrs Fontana was saying. 'I understand,' she said. 'And I promise I won't tell anyone.'

'Good,' Mrs Fontana said. 'Now,' she went on, seeming to produce a piece of paper out of thin air. 'I will give you the Undoing Spell that will turn Twilight back into a pony. Say it when you return home.'

With that, Mrs Fontana handed the paper to Lauren and Lauren read the words:

Twilight Star, Twilight Star,
Twinkling high above so far,
Protect this secret from prying eyes
And return my unicorn to his disguise.
His magical shape is for my eyes only,
Let him be once more a pony.

'Keep Twilight's secret, Lauren,' Mrs Fontana reminded her.

'I will,' Lauren promised.

Twilight bent his knees again and Lauren climbed on to his back. With two bounds he cantered across the grass and rose up into the sky.

'Bye, Mrs Fontana!' Lauren called, catching hold of his mane.

The old lady raised her hand. 'Use the

magic well, my dear,' she called and, with that, she and Walter disappeared into the dark wood.

Twilight and Lauren flew through the sky. Lauren thought she had never felt happier or more excited. There was so much to see. They flew over the woods and rivers, and Mrs Fontana's bookshop, and finally they flew out over the mountains that rose behind Granger's Farm.

At last they returned to the paddock. As they flew down, Lauren suddenly remembered about her parents.

'Twilight!' she gasped. 'I hope Mum and Dad aren't worried about me.'

'Don't worry,' Twilight told her. 'We haven't been gone very long.'

'Oh, Twilight,' Lauren said, 'this is all so exciting!'

Twilight nodded eagerly. 'And the excitement's only just beginning. Soon we'll be having all sorts of adventures together.' He nuzzled her leg. 'Oh, Lauren. I'm so happy you're my Unicorn Friend.'

Lauren hugged him. 'And I'm so happy you're my unicorn.'

As Lauren dismounted, she took the piece of paper that Mrs Fontana had given her out of her pocket. Slowly she read out the Undoing Spell. As she spoke the last word, there was a flash of

blinding purple light and suddenly Lauren felt cold air on her face. She opened her eyes. She was still standing beside Twilight, but he was no longer a unicorn; he was just a small grey pony. For a moment Lauren wondered if she'd imagined everything, but then she looked down at the piece of paper in her hand. No, it had been real.

Twilight snuffled at her hair and she felt a surge of excitement fizz inside her.

'Goodnight,' Lauren whispered, kissing him in delight. Then, picking up the book from the grass, she turned and ran to the house.

As she hurried in, Buddy bounded over to greet her, almost knocking her down in his excitement.

Her dad was washing up the supper dishes at the sink and her mum was pouring Max a drink.

'How was Twilight?' her mum asked.

'He was fine,' Lauren said. 'I . . . I think

I might just go up to my room and read for a while.'

She went upstairs and sat down by her bedroom window. Twilight was grazing in his paddock. Seeming to sense that Lauren was looking at him, he raised his head and whinnied.

A broad grin crept across Lauren's face. Her new pony had turned out to be her secret unicorn.

What adventures they were going to have!

My Secret Unicorn

Dreams Come True

Mel turned Shadow towards the jump. His ears pricked up and he quickened his stride.
'He's going to jump it!' Lauren whispered to Twilight in delight.
Shadow got nearer and nearer, his hooves thudding on the grass.
Then, a metre in front of the jump, he suddenly stopped.

To Iola – dreams really

can come true

CHAPTER One

'It's almost time, Twilight,' Lauren Foster whispered to the grey pony beside her. She looked down at the star-shaped flower in her hand. At the tip of each purple petal, a golden spot glowed. The pony stamped one of his front hooves and pushed at her hand impatiently.

'Just a few more minutes,' Lauren told

him. She looked up. The sun had almost set. This was the moment she'd been waiting for all day. As the last of the sun disappeared behind the mountains, a bright star shone out overhead.

A thrill ran through Lauren. *Now!*

Gently, she began to crumble the petals of the flower between her fingers. As she did so, she whispered the secret words of the Turning Spell.

Twilight Star, Twilight Star,
Twinkling high above so far.
Shining light, shining bright,
Will you grant my wish tonight?
Let my little horse forlorn
Be at last a unicorn!

Almost before the last word had left Lauren's mouth, there was a bright purple flash.

The patch of grass where Twilight had been standing was empty. Lauren looked up. A snow-white unicorn was cantering in circles in the sky.

'Twilight!' Lauren exclaimed in delight.

With a kick of his back legs, Twilight swooped down and landed beside Lauren.

'Hello,' he said, putting his nose close to hers and blowing out softly. Although Twilight's words rang out clearly in Lauren's head, his mouth didn't move. Lauren remembered what he had told her when she had first turned him into a unicorn the night before – as long as she was touching him, or holding a hair from his mane, she would be able to hear him speaking.

Lauren hugged him and then looked down at the petals still clutched in her hand. 'But I didn't throw them on the ground,' she said.

Twilight tossed his flowing silver mane. 'You don't need to any more. The moonflower petals are only needed the *first* time the spell is said. You don't even need the light of the Twilight Star. From now on, all you need to do is say the magic words.' He pawed the grass. 'Come on, Lauren. Let's go flying.'

Lauren didn't need to be asked twice. In a flash, she had scrambled on to his back.

Twilight plunged upwards and Lauren laughed in delight as the wind whipped through her hair. She held on to Twilight's long mane.

'I'm getting better at flying,' Twilight said, cantering in a smooth circle.

'Definitely!' Lauren agreed.

The day before, Twilight's flying had been quite wobbly and she'd been very glad that special unicorn magic had stopped her from falling off! Now she looked down at the fields and woods below.

'Let's fly over the woods,' Twilight said. 'And jump over the treetops.'

'OK,' Lauren agreed. 'But I can't stay

out too long in case Mum and Dad start wondering where I am.'

Twilight turned in the air and headed for the forest that covered the mountains behind Lauren's house.

Lauren could see the nearby farms spread out beneath them. One in particular caught her attention – a white clapboard farmhouse with red barns that hugged the mountainside at the edge of the forest. 'That's Goose Creek Farm,' she said. 'Dad met the man who owns it today. He's called Mr Cassidy. He's got a daughter called Mel who's the same age as me and she's got a pony. Dad's arranged for me to go and visit them tomorrow and you're coming too!'

'Sounds like fun!' Twilight said.

Lauren suddenly looked anxious. 'What if Mel's pony guesses you're a unicorn?' she said. She knew that it was very important no one discovered Twilight's secret. Lauren had been given the spell to turn Twilight into a unicorn by an old lady called Mrs Fontana, and she had told Lauren that she must never let anyone find out Twilight was a unicorn. It might put him in great danger!

'He'll know,' Twilight said, 'but it'll be OK. Horses and ponies understand that a unicorn's secret must be kept.'

'Do all animals know about unicorns?' Lauren asked curiously.

Twilight shook his head. 'Just horses

and ponies, though sometimes other animals will sense I'm different.' He swooped down so that his hooves were skimming the treetops. 'Now, are you ready to do some jumping?'

'You bet!' Lauren exclaimed.

'Then here goes!' Twilight galloped forward through the air and carried her over the top branches of a tall pine tree.

They leapt from one treetop to the next, giddy with excitement. At the far edge of the forest, Twilight cantered into the air and turned a loop-the-loop. Lauren whooped out loud in delight.

All too soon, Lauren realized it was time to go back home. 'If we're much longer, Mum and Dad might start getting worried,' she said to Twilight.

He nodded and they flew back to Granger's Farm.

Twilight landed in his paddock. Lauren dismounted and said the Undoing Spell. There was a bright purple flash as Twilight turned from a unicorn into a small, grey pony.

'See you tomorrow,' Lauren whispered. She gave him a quick hug, then raced back to the house.

Her dad was in the kitchen. He glanced at the kitchen clock. 'You've been out a long time,' he commented.

'I was just playing with Twilight,' Lauren said, her heart pounding.

To her relief, her dad smiled. 'I'm glad

you're enjoying having a pony so much,' he said. 'Life here in the country sure beats life back in the city, doesn't it?'

'Totally,' Lauren agreed happily. It was only a week ago that her family had left their house in the city to move to Granger's Farm, so that Mr Foster could follow his dream of becoming a farmer. But already Lauren felt completely at home.

As Lauren passed her brother's bedroom, she heard laughter. She pushed the door open. Her brother, Max, was in bed and Buddy, Max's Bernese mountain dog puppy, was standing on his hind legs with his big white front paws on the covers. His pink tongue was hanging out and he seemed to be trying to lick every inch of Max's face.

'Honestly, Max, I think he'd get into bed with you if I let him!' Mrs Foster exclaimed as she pushed the black and tan puppy down. 'Buddy, you're a pest,' she scolded, but she smiled as she spoke.

Buddy came gambolling over to Lauren. Not managing to stop in time, he skidded into her legs.

'Oof!' Lauren exclaimed. 'Buddy! You weigh a ton!'

'You wait till he's fully grown,' Mrs Foster said with a laugh. 'Now you'd better get ready for bed too, honey. You and Dad are expected at the Cassidys' house at nine-thirty so you're going to have to be up early to get Twilight fed and groomed in time.'

Lauren nodded.

'I hope you and Mel Cassidy get along,' Mrs Foster went on. 'It would be great for you to have a friend to go riding with.'

'Yeah,' Lauren agreed. 'I hope Mel's nice.'

As she went to her bedroom, she thought about the next day. Would Mel want to be friends with her? Would she want to be friends with Mel? She hoped so.

She got her pyjamas out from under her pillow and walked to her bedroom window. She could see the Blue Ridge

Mountains towering up behind the house and, best of all, she could see Twilight's stable and paddock.

'Goodnight, Twilight,' she whispered, looking at the little pony's shadowy shape grazing by the gate. 'I hope tomorrow's going to be OK.'

Twilight looked up. Lauren was sure she saw him whicker. Blowing him a kiss, she smiled and closed the curtain.

CHAPTER Two

'Buddy! Here, boy!' Max called, crawling under the kitchen table as Lauren ate her cereal the next morning.

Mr Foster was standing by the door talking to Hank and Joe, the two farmhands who helped look after the Fosters' herd of dairy cows and the ten pigs. 'I want to move the calves to the bottom pasture this morning,' Mr Foster was explaining.

Mrs Foster was on the phone. 'Yes, we're finally getting sorted out,' she said, one hand pressed to her ear to shut out the noise in the kitchen.

Lauren got up and put her empty cereal bowl in the dishwasher. 'I'm going to get Twilight ready,' she announced.

The April sun was shining as she stepped outside and the new leaves on the trees looked green and fresh. Lauren breathed in deeply and ran down the path that led from the house to the paddock. Twilight was waiting at the gate. He whinnied when he saw her.

'Hi, fella,' Lauren said, climbing over

the gate. 'I bet you'd like some breakfast.'

Twilight nuzzled her. Snapping the leadrope on to his head-collar, Lauren led him up to his stable and fetched him some pony nuts in a bucket. As he ate, she looked at her watch. Eight-fifteen.

That meant she had an hour to groom him before she and her dad had to leave for the Cassidys' house.

Half an hour later, Lauren stepped back to admire her handiwork. Twilight's scruffy grey coat was looking much cleaner, his hooves gleamed from the hoof oil and his newly washed tail was almost dry.

'You look loads better,' Lauren declared. He whickered in agreement.

'Buddy! Come back!'

Hearing her brother's cry, Lauren looked round. Buddy was galloping down the path towards her, his black ears flopping, his enormous white paws thudding on the grass. Max tore after him.

'Buddy! Careful!' Lauren gasped, as the puppy headed straight for the bucket of water. Buddy tried to stop but he was too late. He crashed into it, sending the dirty suds flying up into the air.

Twilight snorted and jumped back to the end of his rope, but the contents of the bucket splashed all over him.

'Buddy!' Lauren exclaimed. She swung round to Max. He was standing on the path, his hand fixed to his mouth, his blue eyes wide with shock. 'Max!' she cried.

'I'm sorry, I'm really sorry,' Max said. 'I opened the back door and Buddy just ran off down the path. I couldn't stop him, Lauren.'

Lauren sighed. It was no use getting annoyed with Max. It wasn't his fault that Buddy was so clumsy. 'It's OK,' she said. 'I guess I'll just have to groom Twilight again.'

'I'll help you,' Max offered.

Lauren took a towel from the grooming box and handed it to Max. 'Thanks,' she said.

'Look at Buddy,' Max said suddenly.

Lauren looked at the puppy. He was crawling on his tummy towards Twilight, his ears pricked up, his tail wagging like crazy. 'Woof!' he said, jumping back. 'Woof! Woof!' He sat up and cocked his head on one side.

'What's he doing?' Max said in surprise.

'I don't know,' Lauren said with a frown. She tried to move the puppy away, but Buddy just kept staring at Twilight. He seemed fascinated. Lauren felt worried. Could Buddy somehow sense that Twilight wasn't a normal pony? She got hold of Buddy's collar again. 'Here, Max. Maybe you should take him back to the house. Twilight might stand on him by mistake if he gets too close.'

'But what about helping you?' Max said, looking disappointed.

'I'll manage,' Lauren replied quickly. She saw Max's mouth open as if to argue. 'We don't want Buddy to get hurt, do we?'

'No,' Max said, taking Buddy's collar.

As he dragged Buddy back to the house, Lauren bit her lip. If Buddy acted like that in front of her mum and dad, they were bound to get suspicious. She looked at Twilight. He was staring after Buddy, and Lauren was sure he looked concerned.

At nine-fifteen, Lauren rode out of Granger's Farm with her father walking beside Twilight. They headed for Goose Creek Farm. It wasn't far and they were soon walking down the drive towards the house. The back door opened and a tall man with black hair came out on to the veranda.

'Mike!' he said, coming forward to greet Mr Foster. 'Hi. And this must be Lauren. Mel can't wait to meet you. She's with Shadow at the moment – that's her pony. Come on, I'll show you round to the paddock.'

Lauren rode after him. As they reached the back of the house, she saw a paddock with two jumps set out. A dapple-grey pony was tethered to the paddock fence. A girl with black curly hair was standing beside him, brushing his shiny coat.

'Mel!' Mr Cassidy called.

The girl turned. Seeing Lauren, her face lit up with a friendly grin. 'Hi!' she called. Throwing her grooming brush down, she jogged over. 'I'm Mel.'

'I'm Lauren,' Lauren said rather shyly.

'Your pony's gorgeous,' Mel said. 'What's he called?'

'Twilight,' said Lauren, dismounting.

'Twilight.' Mel frowned thoughtfully, patting him. 'Did he used to belong to Jade Roberts?'

'That's right,' Lauren said in surprise.

Mel nodded. 'I thought I recognized him. I go to Pony Club with Jade.' She smiled at Lauren. 'My pony's called Shadow. Do you want to come and meet him?'

Lauren nodded eagerly.

'We'll leave you two girls to get to know each other then,' Mr Cassidy said. 'We'll be in the house if you want us.'

Lauren and Mel nodded. 'So, how long have you had Shadow?' Lauren asked, as she led Twilight over to say hello.

'Six months,' Mel replied. 'I couldn't believe it when Mum and Dad bought him for me. I'd wanted a pony for ... like forever. I think I was born pony-crazy.'

'Me too!' Lauren agreed, grinning at her.

Shadow turned his head to look at Twilight. Lauren held her breath. What if he acted as strangely as Buddy had?

But, after staring at Twilight for a moment, Shadow simply snorted softly and stretched out his muzzle to say hello.

Twilight blew down his nostrils in reply.

'They like each other!' Mel said. She beamed at Lauren. 'It's going to be so cool being neighbours – I can just tell!'

Happiness welled up inside Lauren.

'I'll get Shadow tacked up,' Mel said. 'Then we can play catch in the paddock.'

Lauren and Mel had great fun. Shadow was fast and could turn very quickly, but Twilight was also pretty speedy. They chased each other round the paddock, trying to tag each other, and then they had an egg-and-spoon race, a trotting race and a race where they had to canter around poles stuck in the ground in a line. 'This is loads better than riding on my own!' Mel said as they finished in a dead heat.

'Shall we jump next?' Lauren asked, looking at the fences.

Mel's face fell. 'There's no point,' she

sighed. 'Shadow doesn't jump. I took him to a Pony Club mounted meeting last month but he wouldn't even go near a jump. Watch.'

She cantered Shadow away from Twilight and turned him towards one of the fences. He slowed to a trot and then to a walk. Mel kicked his sides but it made no difference. He stopped a metre away from the jump.

'He does it every time,' Mel said, riding back to Lauren. 'And I don't know what I'm going to do. There's another mounted meeting this Saturday and Jade Roberts and her friend Monica were really mean about him when he wouldn't jump last time.'

'Maybe he'll follow Twilight over a jump,' Lauren suggested.

But even when Twilight jumped, Shadow refused to follow. As soon as Mel turned him towards the fences, he slowed down, his ears back.

'It's no use,' Mel sighed. 'He's not going to do it.' She patted Shadow. 'It doesn't matter, Shadow,' she said. 'I love you whether you can jump or not.'

Although Mel tried to smile, Lauren could see the sadness in her new friend's eyes. 'I'll try to think of some other way to help,' Lauren promised. 'If I come over tomorrow after school, maybe we could try again then.'

'That would be great,' Mel said, looking

more cheerful. 'Between the two of us we must be able to think of something.'

They untacked the ponies and turned them out into the paddock to graze. Then Mel showed Lauren around Goose Creek Farm. Just up the track from the barn with Shadow's stall was an enormous red hay-barn. In it was Mel's cat, Sparkle. 'She's just had two kittens,' Mel said to Lauren. 'They're only three weeks old.'

Lauren gasped in delight as she saw the two tiny black kittens snuggled into their mother's side. Sparkle had made a nest in a pile of loose hay at the back of the barn and the two kittens were sleeping beside her.

'What have you called them?' Lauren asked in a low voice.

'Star and Midnight,' Mel whispered back. 'Mum and Dad have said I can keep them both.'

As they walked back down the path towards the paddock and the farmhouse, Mel turned to Lauren. 'You know, you should join Pony Club too. We have mounted and unmounted meetings every month, competitions and there's even a camp in the summer!'

Lauren hesitated, thinking about the two girls who had been mean to Mel.

Mel seemed to read her mind. 'It's only Jade and Monica who are like that,' she said. 'The others in my group are really nice.'

'OK then,' Lauren agreed. 'I'll ask.'

'You two look like you've been having fun,' Mr Foster said, as Lauren and Mel ran into the large kitchen. He and Mr Cassidy were sitting at the table, having coffee.

'We have!' Lauren exclaimed. 'We went riding and then Mel showed me round, and she wants to know if I can join her Pony Club.' She looked at Mel, who nodded eagerly.

'We could go to the meetings together. It would be cool!' Lauren added. 'Can I join, Dad?'

Mr Foster smiled. 'It sounds like a great idea.'

'I've got the secretary's number somewhere here,' Mr Cassidy said, getting up and rummaging through a pile of papers by the telephone. 'Yes, here we are.' He wrote it down on a piece of paper and handed it to Mr Foster. 'It's a good Pony Club. The kids learn a lot there. There's a mounted meeting next weekend. Lauren and Twilight are very welcome to have a ride there in our trailer.'

'Thanks,' said Mr Foster, taking the paper from him. 'I'll ring the secretary when we get home.'

Lauren and Mel exchanged delighted looks.

'I'm so glad you've moved here,' Mel said, as Lauren got back on Twilight to ride home.

'Me too,' Lauren said, grinning at her.

'Come on, then,' Mr Foster said, patting Twilight's neck. 'Let's go.'

Mel ran along the driveway with them. 'I'll see you at school tomorrow,' she called, as Lauren rode out of the drive.

'So do you like Mel, then?' Mr Foster said to Lauren, as they walked along the road.

'Yeah!' Lauren said. 'She's lots of fun.' She stroked Twilight's neck. She couldn't stop thinking about Shadow's jumping problem. She really wanted to be able to help. But how?

Maybe Twilight will know, she thought.

CHAPTER Three

After supper, Lauren pulled on her trainers. The sun had just set and she was anxious to get moving. 'I'm just going to check on Twilight,' she said to her mum.

'OK, honey,' Mrs Foster said. 'But don't be out for too long. Remember you've got school starting tomorrow.'

Buddy ran to the door and stood

there, his head cocked on one side.

'You're not coming with me, Buddy,' Lauren told him. She went outside, shutting the door carefully behind her, and hurried down the path to the paddock. Would Twilight be able to think of a way to help Shadow?

Twilight whickered when he saw her. Lauren began to say the words of the Turning Spell:

Twilight Star, Twilight Star ...

Suddenly Twilight whinnied loudly.

Lauren stopped. He seemed to be staring at something over her shoulder. She swung round to see what it was.

Buddy was standing on the path behind her.

'Buddy! Go away!' Lauren exclaimed. Buddy was curious enough about Twilight already. If he saw Twilight change into a unicorn, he would never leave him alone. She took hold of the puppy's collar.

'Buddy!' she heard her dad shouting.

'He's here, Dad!' Lauren called back.

Mr Foster came down the path. 'I only opened the door for a second. Buddy just raced off after you. Come on, fella,' he said, taking hold of the puppy's collar. 'You come in with me.'

Lauren waited until she heard the door of the house shut and then she whispered the secret words.

There was a purple flash and suddenly Twilight was standing before her, a snow-white unicorn once again.

'That was close,' he said.

'I know,' Lauren said, feeling worried. 'I'm going to have to be so careful. Buddy's far too interested in you.' Suddenly she remembered what she'd been going to ask Twilight. 'Do you know why Shadow won't jump? Mel's really upset about it.'

'I don't know,' Twilight admitted. He pawed the grass. 'But we could visit him and find out.'

'Now?' Lauren said, looking at the sky. It still wasn't properly dark yet. 'But what if Mel or her parents see us?'

'We could go later then,' Twilight said.

Lauren hesitated. 'Well, I guess I could come just after I go to bed,' she said. 'Mum's writing a new book so she'll be working on her computer and Dad's bound to be watching TV. But I won't be able to stay out long.'

'We'll be quick,' Twilight promised.

'All right then,' Lauren agreed. 'I'll come back as soon as I can.' She said the Undoing Spell, turning Twilight back into a pony, and hurried back to the house.

After her mum had said goodnight and gone into her study to work, Lauren pulled her jeans on over her pyjamas and scribbled a quick note for her parents just in case they came to check on her and were worried.

I'll be back soon. I've just gone to see Twilight.
Lots of love, Lauren XXX

Leaving it on her bed, she crept down the stairs and out of the house.

I'll be back as quickly as I can, she told herself as she hurried down to the paddock.

It only took a few seconds to change Twilight into a unicorn. 'Quick!' Lauren said. She scrambled on to his back. 'Let's go!'

They swooped down on Shadow's paddock at Goose Creek Farm. 'There he is!' Lauren said, spotting the dark shape of Mel's dapple-grey pony.

Twilight landed with a soft whicker just behind him. Shadow swung round with an alarmed snort.

Twilight whinnied and Lauren saw Shadow relax. He whinnied back as if he was talking to Twilight.

'What's he saying?' Lauren asked Twilight.

'That he knew I was a unicorn,' Twilight said. 'And he would like to know why we've come.'

Lauren didn't want to waste any time. 'Ask him why he won't jump,' she said to Twilight.

'He understands you,' Twilight told her as Shadow whinnied in reply. Twilight listened to the dapple-grey pony for a few moments. 'He's scared,' he told Lauren. 'He says that when he was a foal, he was jumping over a tree trunk with the other foals in his field and he banged his legs really hard. Ever since then, he's been afraid of jumping. He hates making Mel upset but he just can't do it.'

'Have you got any magical powers that could help him not to feel so scared, Twilight?' Lauren asked.

'I don't know,' Twilight replied doubtfully. 'I know I've got some magical powers, but I'm not sure what they are. I guess I might be able to help, but I don't know how.'

Lauren felt disappointed. She'd been hoping that Twilight would be able to do some magic and make everything OK. She thought hard. If they couldn't use Twilight's powers to help Shadow then maybe she could come up with a more practical solution. 'If I put the poles from the jumps on the ground do you think you might be able to walk over them?' she asked Shadow.

Shadow snorted.

'He says he might,' Twilight translated.

'Well, that would be a start,' Lauren said. She got off Twilight's back and took two poles and laid them out on the grass. *It's lucky that Shadow's paddock is hidden from the farmhouse,* she thought.

'Try walking over these,' she said to Shadow. 'At least it's a step towards jumping.'

Shadow looked very nervous.

'It'll be OK,' Twilight encouraged him.

Shadow walked up to the first pole and stopped. Then, snorting loudly, he stepped over it, picking his hooves up high.

'Well done!' Lauren cried. 'Now try the other one, Shadow.'

The same thing happened.

'You did it!' Twilight exclaimed as Shadow trotted back to them, suddenly

looking much happier.

'I'll put up a tiny jump now,' Lauren said. 'Let's see if you can do that.'

But Shadow backed off, whinnying.

Twilight sighed. 'He doesn't want to. He's still too frightened to try a jump.' Shadow neighed. 'If we can come and help him some more, he might get braver.'

It was better than nothing. 'OK, we'll come again tomorrow,' Lauren said. She gave Shadow a hug and then got back on to Twilight. 'We'll help you, Shadow. No matter how long it takes.'

CHAPTER Four

'Come on, Lauren!' Mrs Foster called the next morning.

Lauren checked her reflection for the last time in her bedroom mirror. She was wearing new jeans and a blue T-shirt. Her freshly washed hair was tied back in a ponytail. She swallowed nervously. Her first day at a new school. What was it going to be like?

Taking a deep breath, she ran downstairs. Her mum and Max were waiting by the door.

'Feeling nervous?' Mrs Foster asked her.

'A little,' Lauren admitted, yawning.

Her mum frowned. 'Didn't you sleep well last night?'

'I'm fine, Mum,' Lauren said quickly. She'd got back into the house safely after her adventure with Twilight and she didn't want her mum getting suspicious now. She picked up her school bag. 'Come on. Let's go.'

Silver River Elementary School was only a ten-minute drive away from Granger's Farm. It was a low brick building. As

★ *Dreams Come True* ★

Mrs Foster parked the car, Lauren saw Mel standing at the school gates. 'There's Mel!' she exclaimed.

She jumped out of the car and ran over. 'Hi!'

'Hi!' Mel said. 'I thought I'd wait for you.'

Mrs Foster and Max walked up to them. 'This is my mum and my brother, Max,' Lauren said.

'Pleased to meet you,' Mel said politely. 'I'm in the same class as Lauren, Mrs Foster. I can show her there if you want.'

Mrs Foster looked questioningly at Lauren, who nodded. 'Yeah, I'll be fine, Mum,' she said quickly.

'Well, in that case,' Mrs Foster said,

'that would be a real help, Mel. It gives me more time to get Max settled into his classroom. I'll stop by the office, Lauren, and tell them you're here.'

'Bye, Mum,' said Lauren, giving her a quick kiss. 'I'll see you this afternoon.'

Mrs Foster nodded. 'I'll pick you up here at the gates. Have a good day, honey.'

'She will,' Mel said, swinging her school bag on to her shoulder. 'Come on, Lauren. I want to show you around.'

By morning break, Lauren's nerves had totally disappeared. Mr Noland, her new teacher, was strict but fun. Even better, he'd let her and Mel sit together. The other kids in the class seemed really keen to be friends too – all apart from Jade Roberts and her friend Monica Corder. They hadn't said a word to Lauren or Mel, although they had giggled when Jade had leaned over Mel's desk and caught sight of a horse that Mel had drawn.

'Looks more like a pig than a horse,' Jade had said to Monica.

'Or a mule,' Monica had said, flicking her blonde hair back.

'Just like her dumb pony,' Jade went on, her green eyes looking mockingly at Mel. 'I mean, imagine having a dumb pony that won't jump. How sad can you get?'

'He's not dumb!' Lauren said angrily.

Jade turned her full attention to her. 'And what do *you* know about horses?'

'Well, I've got one,' Lauren said.

'Lauren Foster?' Jade said suddenly. 'You're the girl who owns Twilight, aren't you?' When Lauren nodded, Jade laughed. 'How sad. I got my dad to sell him because he wasn't good enough to win ribbons. My new pony, Prince, is a hundred times better.'

Lauren glared at them but, before she could say anything, Mr Noland heard the whispering and told Jade and Monica to be quiet.

Lauren was still fuming when the lesson came to an end.

'Come on, Lauren!' Mel said as they went outside. 'Let's go and sit under the tree. I've brought some photos of

Shadow to show you.'

'You know, I had an idea last night,' Lauren said quickly, wanting to cheer her up. 'I think Shadow might be scared of jumping . . . for some reason. We could try walking him over poles on the ground, then, as he gets braver, we could put up some tiny jumps.'

Mel looked doubtful. 'Do you really think it will work?'

'I'm sure,' Lauren said. 'Look, why don't I come over after school with Twilight and we can try then?'

Her enthusiasm seemed to encourage Mel.

'OK,' she said eagerly. 'Let's do it.'

CHAPTER Five

'Should I try now?' Mel said to Lauren later that afternoon. She was mounted on Shadow and nervously looking at the poles that she and Lauren had laid out on the grass.

'Yes,' Lauren said, patting Twilight. 'Just trot him over them.'

Mel turned Shadow towards the poles. The little dapple-grey pony glanced once at Twilight, and then trotted bravely over them.

'He did it!' Mel exclaimed in astonishment.

'I told you!' Lauren said. 'Now try again.'

So Mel did. By the time Shadow had trotted and cantered over the poles ten times, Mel was beaming from ear to ear. 'Maybe I'll be able to get him to jump in the end,' she said. She got off Shadow and hugged him. 'You're such a good boy!'

Shadow snorted and Lauren was sure that he looked pleased.

After untacking the ponies and turning them out into Shadow's paddock to graze, Lauren and Mel went up the path to see Sparkle and her two kittens in the barn.

Star and Midnight were awake. They were toddling round the nest of hay, their heads looking almost too large for their fluffy black bodies.

'Which one's which?' Lauren asked. They looked identical to her.

'Star's got a white star shape on her tummy,' Mel explained. She picked up the kitten nearest her. 'Look.'

'Oh, yes!' Lauren laughed, seeing the white hairs.

'Do you want to hold her?' Mel asked.

Lauren nodded eagerly and Mel handed Star over. The little kitten looked

into Lauren's face and then miaowed, her mouth opening so wide that Lauren could see all the way to the back of her pink throat. 'Hello,' Lauren murmured. 'Aren't you lovely?' Star cuddled into her arms.

'Wasn't Shadow good today?' Mel said to Lauren as she picked up Midnight.

'Yes, he was,' Lauren said. 'I'm sure he'll learn to jump in the end.'

'I hope so,' said Mel. 'I just wish he could learn in time for the meeting on Saturday. Jade and Monica are being so mean about him and the only thing that's going to stop them is if he learns to jump.' She looked at Lauren hopefully. 'Do you think we might have him jumping soon?'

'We might,' Lauren said. 'Fingers crossed.'

As Lauren rode Twilight home, she couldn't stop thinking about Mel's words.

Shadow might be able to learn to jump with help, but how long would that take? It might take ages and Mel would just continue to get teased.

If only we could teach him to jump more quickly, Lauren thought.

She remembered what Twilight had said about his powers – he had some but he didn't know what they were. Maybe he did have some magic that could help. But how could they find out?

And then the answer came to her. *Mrs Fontana.* Mrs Fontana was the only other person in the world who knew Twilight's secret. She'd told Lauren that unicorns existed and had given Lauren an old book that contained the words of the

Turning Spell. If anyone would be able to help, she would.

As soon as she got home, Lauren ran into the house. Her mum was working on her computer.

'Mum,' Lauren said, 'can you take me to Mrs Fontana's bookshop?'

Mrs Foster frowned. 'Why?'

Lauren didn't know what to say. 'I . . . I want to ask Mrs Fontana something,' she said. 'It's for a project I'm doing. I thought Mrs Fontana might be able to help.'

'Well, actually I was going to go into town,' Mrs Foster said. 'I need to get some film for the camera. Max wants to take some photos of Buddy to show to his teacher. You could go and see Mrs Fontana while I pick up the film.'

'Great!' Lauren said.

'Get changed then,' Mrs Foster said. 'We'll go right now.'

Almost before Mrs Foster had parked, Lauren scrambled out of the car.

'I'll meet you there,' Mrs Foster said. 'Don't go anywhere else.'

'Don't worry, I won't,' Lauren promised.

She raced over to the bookshop with its brown and gold sign. A chime jangled as she pushed open the door. There was the familiar rose-patterned carpet on the floor and the air smelled faintly of blackcurrants. Books spilled off every shelf and surface.

Walter, Mrs Fontana's terrier, came trotting over as soon as Lauren walked inside. 'Hi, boy,' Lauren said, bending down to pat him. As she straightened up, she saw that the old lady had appeared, as if by magic. Mrs Fontana's face was lined and wrinkled but her blue eyes shone out, bright and clear. She had a mustard-yellow shawl clasped loosely around her shoulders and her long grey hair was pinned up in a bun.

'Hello, Lauren,' she said. 'What can I do for you today?'

Lauren hesitated. It was so hard to

launch straight into a discussion about unicorns in broad daylight. 'Well . . . er . . .'

Mrs Fontana looked over her shoulder to where a couple of people were browsing along a bookshelf. 'Come down to the children's section,' she said softly. 'Walter will tell me if I'm needed.'

The black and white terrier jumped up on to the counter by the till and sat down, his ears pricked. It was as if he'd understood every word Mrs Fontana had said.

Lauren followed Mrs Fontana to the children's section at one side of the shop. There was an armchair and cushions on the floor. 'So how's Twilight?' Mrs Fontana said, sitting down.

'Fine,' Lauren replied. She lowered her voice. 'We're trying to help this pony, Mrs Fontana. He belongs to my friend and he's scared of jumping.' She quickly explained about Shadow. 'He's so scared that it might take ages to get him jumping properly,' she said. 'Do you know if Twilight has any magical powers that could help?'

Mrs Fontana smiled. 'Twilight has many magical powers, Lauren. But I cannot tell you what they are. A unicorn has to discover his powers for himself.' She leaned forward and took Lauren's hands in hers. 'Don't worry, Twilight *is* able to help this pony,' she said. 'But it is up to you to help him work out how,

Lauren. You became a Unicorn Friend because you have a good heart and the imagination to believe in magic. Use those qualities and together you and Twilight will discover his powers.'

Letting go of Lauren's hands, she straightened up. Her face looked less serious now. 'So,' she said, her eyes crinkling up at the corners in a smile, 'has Buddy found out Twilight's secret yet?'

Lauren stared at her. How had Mrs Fontana known about the problems she was having with Buddy?

Mrs Fontana seemed to sense her astonishment. 'When I was a Unicorn Friend I had a dog who was very curious about my unicorn,' she explained. 'He almost found my secret out several times.'

'You had your own unicorn?' Lauren gasped. She'd known that Mrs Fontana had seen a unicorn, but the old lady had never told her that she too had once been a Unicorn Friend.

'I did,' Mrs Fontana said softly. 'A long time ago.'

A hundred questions bubbled up inside Lauren. What had Mrs Fontana's unicorn been like? What had it been called? How had Mrs Fontana discovered that it was a unicorn? And, most of all, what had happened to it? Why didn't Mrs Fontana have it any more?

But before she could ask any of these questions, Walter barked.

'A customer must need help,' Mrs Fontana said, getting to her feet. She smiled at Lauren. 'Good luck with Shadow, Lauren. I hope you and Twilight can find a way to help, and be careful with Buddy. Try not to let him find out Twilight's secret.'

With that, Mrs Fontana went to the front of the shop where someone was waiting to pay for their books.

The shop door opened and Mrs Foster walked in. Lauren ran over. 'Hi, Mum.'

'Are you ready to go?' Mrs Foster asked.

Lauren nodded. 'Bye, Mrs Fontana,' she

said, glancing over to the desk where the old woman was wrapping up the customer's purchases.

Mrs Fontana looked up. 'Goodbye, Lauren,' she said. She smiled. 'And good luck.'

CHAPTER Six

That evening, Lauren crept out of the house again.

'Are we going to see Shadow?' Twilight asked.

'Yes. Let's be quick,' Lauren said, getting on to his back.

As they flew to Goose Creek Farm, she told him what Mrs Fontana had said. 'You have got powers that can help,' she told him.

'But how can I use them if I don't know what they are?' Twilight said.

'I don't know,' Lauren admitted. She'd been thinking the same thing ever since she'd left Mrs Fontana's shop.

Shadow was waiting for them. He whinnied.

'You were great today, Shadow!' Twilight said as he landed.

Shadow bowed his head, as if a bit embarrassed by the praise. He snorted.

'He wants to know if he should have another go at trotting over the poles,' Twilight told Lauren.

'What about trying a small jump?' Lauren suggested hopefully.

Shadow looked worried.

'Go on, just have a go,' Twilight said.

Shadow hesitated for a moment and then slowly nodded his head.

Before Shadow could change his mind, Lauren scrambled off Twilight and put up a tiny jump. 'You can do it, Shadow!' she said.

Shadow nodded his head and, turning towards the jump, he began to trot.

'He's going to do it!' Lauren gasped to Twilight.

But then Shadow stopped dead.

'Oh dear,' Lauren sighed.

She and Twilight trotted over. Shadow was standing a few metres away from the jump. 'What went wrong?' Lauren asked him. 'Why did you stop?'

The dapple-grey pony hung his head and snorted sadly.

'He was just too scared,' Twilight told Lauren.

Shadow looked so dejected that Lauren was sure that if ponies could cry, he would have been in tears.

Twilight stepped forward and touched his glowing horn to Shadow's neck. 'It's OK,' Lauren heard him say softly. 'You tried your best. Don't be upset.'

They stood there for a moment, and then Lauren saw the little dapple-grey pony's ears flicker forward. He raised his head and whickered in a surprised sort of way.

'What's he saying?' Lauren asked Twilight.

'That he's feeling a bit better,' Twilight replied.

Shadow whickered again.

'Much better,' Twilight said.

Lauren saw Shadow look at the jump. His eyes suddenly seemed to be full of confidence. He whinnied.

'In fact, he says he feels so much better that he thinks he might be able to clear the jump,' Twilight said, looking astonished.

Shadow pricked up his ears and trotted away from them. Turning towards the jump, he started to canter. Lauren and Twilight watched in amazement as he flew over it.

'He jumped it!' Lauren exclaimed.

Shadow came cantering back to them, whinnying.

'He says that when we were talking he suddenly felt really brave,' Twilight said,

stamping his front hoof in excitement. 'He says he's never felt like that before, but it was as if he just knew he could do it.'

Shadow nuzzled Twilight and suddenly Lauren's eyes widened. 'Your horn!' she exclaimed to Twilight. 'You were touching him with your horn when he started to feel brave. Perhaps that's one of your magical powers. Maybe by touching him you gave him your courage – a unicorn's bravery.'

Shadow tossed his head and whinnied.

'He says he doesn't care what happened, he's just glad that he could do it,' Twilight said.

Shadow nodded his head, and then he turned and cantered over the jump again.

Lauren hugged Twilight in delight. 'This is brilliant!' she said. 'Mel is going to be so pleased.' Her heart sang. She couldn't wait to see her friend's face when she jumped Shadow tomorrow!

*

Lauren was even more pleased by their night's work when Jade started teasing Mel again the next day at lunchtime.

'Still planning on going to the meeting on Saturday, are you, Mel?' Jade asked, coming over to them as they put their trays away. 'I don't know why you're bothering. It's not like Shadow will jump. Can't your parents afford to buy you a better pony?'

'Mel doesn't want another pony,' Lauren said, unable to bear their teasing a second longer. 'Shadow's fine.'

Jade laughed. 'Yeah, right,' she said, walking off laughing.

Lauren looked at her friend. Mel was biting her lip in frustration. 'I hate her!'

she burst out. 'I think I'm just going to tell Dad that I don't want to go on Saturday.'

'You can't,' Lauren said. 'You've got to come, Mel. If you don't, Jade and Monica will tease you again next week.' Mel looked even more miserable. 'Shadow will be good,' Lauren went on. 'In fact, when you ride him today I'm sure he's going to jump.'

Mel looked at her doubtfully. 'You think so?'

'I know so,' Lauren said confidently.

As soon as Lauren got home after school, she gave Twilight a quick brush over and rode him round to Mel's. 'I can't wait to see her face when Shadow jumps,' Lauren said to him, as they trotted along the road.

Mel was just putting Shadow's saddle on when they arrived. When they rode into the paddock, Lauren set up the jump exactly as she had done the night before.

Then she got back on Twilight. 'Try Shadow now!' she called to Mel.

'OK,' Mel said. She turned Shadow towards the jump. His ears pricked up and he quickened his stride.

'He's going to jump it!' Lauren whispered to Twilight in delight.

Shadow got nearer and nearer, his hooves thudding on the grass.

Then, a metre in front of the jump, he suddenly stopped.

CHAPTER Seven

Lauren gasped in disappointment. After last night, she'd been sure that Shadow was going to jump the fence.

Twilight snorted and Lauren knew he was just as surprised as she was that Shadow had stopped.

Mel turned the dapple-grey pony away from the jump. 'I'll try him again,' she called. 'It almost felt like he was going to jump it then.' But when she tried again, Shadow wouldn't go anywhere near the fence.

Mel rode back to Lauren looking bitterly disappointed. 'I guess I should have known better than to think he would jump it,' she said. Shadow hung his head sadly. Mel hugged him. 'Don't worry, boy. I still love you.'

Despite her words, Shadow looked very upset. He didn't prick his ears up once, not even when they played catch.

'I think I'll take him in,' Mel said at last. 'He doesn't seem very happy.'

Lauren nodded. 'I'm sorry, Mel,' she said, as they dismounted.

'It's not your fault,' Mel said with a sigh.

Lauren didn't hang around for long. She had a feeling that Mel wanted to be on her own and so, after a bit, she got back on to Twilight and rode him home.

'What went wrong?' she said to him. 'Why didn't Shadow jump?'

Twilight shook his head and snorted.

'I'll come down to your paddock tonight,' Lauren told him. 'We've got to sort this out.'

She was grooming Twilight back at Granger's Farm when Buddy came running down the path towards them. He skidded to a stop and began to sniff around Twilight's hooves.

'Buddy, go away!' Lauren said.

Buddy sat down and, cocking his head on one side, he whined at Twilight.

Just then, Max came running down the path. 'There you are, Buddy!' he said, as the puppy trotted over to meet him. Buddy licked his hand and then turned back to Twilight and woofed.

Max frowned. 'Why does Buddy act so weird around Twilight, Lauren?'

'I don't know,' Lauren said. 'Look, I'm trying to groom him. Why don't you take Buddy for a walk, Max?'

But Max didn't seem to be listening. Suddenly his eyes widened as he looked at Twilight. 'Maybe Twilight's an alien, Lauren!' he gasped.

'An alien!' Lauren stared at him.

'Yeah, maybe Twilight's an alien from another planet. He's in disguise so that he can spy on us and Buddy knows it.'

'Don't be dumb, Max. Twilight's just a pony,' Lauren said, desperately trying to act as if Max was totally crazy.

'So why does Buddy act so weird around him, then?' Max said.

'Because . . . because he's not used to horses,' Lauren said quickly.

But Max didn't look convinced. 'I'm going to tell Mum,' he said and, turning, he ran back up the path.

Lauren stared after him. She was sure her mum would just laugh at Max's idea about aliens, but the last thing she wanted was Max going on and on saying that there was something odd about Twilight.

'You see all the trouble you're causing?' she said to Buddy, who was sniffing at Twilight's tail.

CHAPTER Eight

It was Lauren's turn to help wash the dishes after supper. Once they were all dried and put away, she pulled on her boots. 'I'm going to see Twilight, Mum,' she said.

'OK,' Mrs Foster said. She looked round. 'Has anyone seen Max?'

Lauren and her dad shook their heads.

Mrs Foster smiled. 'He's probably in

his room drawing aliens.'

'Or Twilight's spaceship,' Mr Foster said with a laugh.

Lauren let herself out of the back door, feeling very relieved that her mum and dad were treating her brother's suspicions as a joke.

'Hi, boy,' she called, as Twilight whinnied to her from the paddock gate. 'Do you know why Shadow wouldn't jump today?' she asked Twilight as soon as she had turned him into a unicorn.

'No,' Twilight replied.

'Let's go and see him,' Lauren said. 'There has to be a reason.'

Twilight flew to Shadow's field. The little dapple-grey pony was standing quietly, still looking very unhappy.

'Oh, Shadow,' Lauren said, sliding off Twilight's back and going over to him. 'What went wrong today? Why couldn't you jump?'

Shadow whinnied.

'Oh,' Twilight said. He turned to Lauren. 'Poor Shadow. He says he really wanted to, but he just didn't feel brave enough without the touch of my horn.'

Shadow neighed sadly.

Lauren didn't like to see Shadow looking so upset. 'I don't know what to do,' she told Shadow. 'You know Twilight can't be a unicorn when there are other people around.'

Shadow nodded.

He didn't try jumping again that evening. After all, they knew he *could* jump at night when Twilight was a unicorn – it was jumping in the day that was the problem.

Lauren sighed unhappily as she and

Twilight flew home. She really wished there was something they could do to help.

The next morning at school, Mel looked serious. 'I've decided that I'm not going to try and jump Shadow ever again,' she told Lauren. 'It just makes him so miserable and I'd rather get teased than make him unhappy.'

'What will you do about the meeting on Saturday?' Lauren asked.

'I'll have to say that I don't want to jump him.' Mel glanced across the classroom to where Jade and Monica were sitting. 'And I'll just have to put up with whatever those two say.'

Lauren squeezed her arm comfortingly. 'Take no notice of them.'

'Easier said than done,' Mel sighed. She forced a smile on her face. 'Will you still come over with Twilight this afternoon though? We could go for a trail ride.'

Lauren nodded. 'Sure,' she said.

When Lauren got to Goose Creek Farm that afternoon, Mel was already mounted on Shadow. 'We'd better get going,' Mel said. 'Mum thinks there might be a storm coming.'

Lauren looked up at the overcast sky. The air certainly had a heavy, stormy feel about it.

They rode up the path towards the

woods. Mr Cassidy was fixing a fence near to the hay-barn. 'Don't go out too far,' he called.

'We'll stay close to the farm,' Mel promised. 'Come on, Lauren! Let's go.'

They urged Shadow and Twilight into a trot.

'Let's go into the woods,' Mel said. 'There's a great trail there with a sandy bit where we can have a canter.'

'OK,' Lauren said, shortening Twilight's reins. His ears flickered back and forth. 'Come on, boy,' she said encouragingly.

A few minutes later, they entered the woods. The tops of the tall trees met over their heads like a green ceiling. Lauren smiled to herself. What would Mel say if she knew that Twilight had jumped over those very treetops with Lauren on his back?

'Here's the long canter,' Mel said. The trail stretched out in front of them, straight and inviting. 'Are you ready?'

Lauren nodded.

Mel leaned forward and gave Shadow his head. The dapple-grey pony bounded into a canter. Twilight hesitated for a moment and then, when Lauren squeezed his side, he followed.

The wind whipped against Lauren's face as she leaned forward and urged Twilight on. His hooves thudded down on the sand and she could feel a broad grin stretch across her face. This was as good as flying!

At last, the trail began to narrow and they slowed Twilight and Shadow to a trot and then to a walk. Both ponies were breathing hard from the canter, so Lauren and Mel let them walk for a while.

Suddenly, they heard a deep, low rumbling noise. The leaves on the branches nearest to them seemed to shiver slightly.

'Thunder!' Mel said, looking at Lauren in alarm. 'We'd better turn around.'

As they began to trot back along the trail, they heard a pitter-pattering of rain on the leafy canopy above them.

Mel nodded and Shadow and Twilight began to canter along the path. Lauren felt worried. Her parents had warned her lots of times about not being out in a thunderstorm.

As they reached the entrance to the woods, Lauren reined Twilight in. A jagged flash of lightning forked down, lighting up the darkened sky.

'Maybe we should stay here,' Mel stammered, looking frightened.

'No, it's really dangerous to stay near trees,' Lauren said. 'The lightning might strike one of them.' She looked down the path towards the house. 'If we gallop, we'll be back in a minute,' she said, looking at the lights shining invitingly out of the farmhouse's windows. 'Come on!'

She leaned forward and Twilight plunged out from the trees.

'Come on, Twilight,' Lauren urged, leaning low over his neck like a jockey. Twilight's hooves pounded as he galloped down the track, passing the hay-barn and heading towards the barn with Shadow's stall.

Suddenly, Lauren saw Mel's dad standing in the barn's entrance.

Reaching Mr Cassidy, Twilight skidded to a halt. Shadow was only a metre behind.

'Quick!' Mr Cassidy shouted above the noise of the storm. 'Get into the barn before the rain gets any heavier!'

Lauren and Mel flung themselves off

Twilight and Shadow's backs and ran with them inside.

'I've never seen a storm blow up so quickly,' Mr Cassidy said.

Suddenly, there was a clap of thunder and at the same time the sky outside lit up with a bright white flash of lightning. There was a loud bang nearby.

Mr Cassidy ran to the entrance and looked out. 'A tree by the hay-barn's been hit. It's on fire!' he exclaimed. 'I'm going to have to call the fire department. You stay here while I go to the house. I don't want you outside in this.'

'But what about the fire?' Mel cried.

'It's all right. It won't reach you here,' Mr Cassidy said. 'I'll be back as soon as I can.' And with that, he ducked his head and ran out.

Lauren led Twilight to the entrance and looked up the track towards the hay-barn. The tall oak tree that stood next to it was burning brightly.

Mel joined her. 'If it falls, the whole barn will go up in flames! Dad had better be . . .' She broke off, her eyes widening. 'Sparkle!' she cried in horror. 'Lauren! Sparkle and her kittens are inside!'

CHAPTER Nine

Mel put her foot in the stirrup and swung herself up on to Shadow's back.

'What are you doing?' Lauren exclaimed.

'I've got to save Sparkle,' Mel said, digging her heels into Shadow's sides and heading out.

'It's too dangerous, Mel!' Lauren cried.

But it was too late. Mel was already

cantering Shadow up the track towards the barn.

Lauren didn't hesitate. Swinging herself up on Twilight's back, she galloped after her friend. 'Mel! Stop!' she yelled. She hated the thought of Sparkle and the kittens being trapped in the barn, but she knew Mel's life could be in danger if she went inside.

But Mel didn't listen. She urged Shadow past the burning tree and up to the barn door. Jumping off his back, she hauled it open.

Sparkle came racing out. She was carrying one of the kittens in her mouth. Lauren saw a flash of white on the kitten's tummy. Star! But what about

Midnight? He must still be inside.

To her horror, Lauren saw Mel loop Shadow's reins over her arm and run into the barn.

Twilight gave an alarmed whinny. There was a loud creak. Lauren looked up. A huge burning branch of the oak tree looked as if it was about to break off.

'Mel!' she shouted. 'Get out!'

Mel appeared on foot in the doorway of the barn, clutching Midnight.

'Quick!' Lauren yelled, looking up at the tree.

But it was too late. Before Mel could get out of the barn, there was a loud crack and the burning branch crashed to the ground in front of the barn door.

Mel screamed and Lauren gasped. The branch was blocking the way out!

Lauren could just see Mel's terrified

eyes through the smoke that was filling the air. There was only one way for her to get out.

'Get up on Shadow and make him jump the branch, Mel!' Lauren cried. 'It's the only way.'

'But he won't do it!' Mel shouted.

'Just try!' Lauren called.

Clutching Midnight to her chest, Mel scrambled on to Shadow's back.

Lauren glanced around, desperately hoping to see Mr Cassidy or the fire department arriving, but there was no one there. 'Shadow, please!' she yelled, as Mel began to trot him towards the log. 'You've got to jump it! For Mel!'

She heard Shadow neigh uncertainly

through the smoke. *Please jump it,* Lauren prayed. *You might not have Twilight's magical powers to help you, but you can still do it. Please, Shadow, please!*

She saw Shadow hesitate and dread gripped her heart. He wasn't going to be able to do it.

'Melanie!' Hearing a hoarse cry, Lauren swung round. Mr Cassidy was running up the hill towards them, looking horrified. For a moment, Lauren felt a surge of hope but then her heart plummeted. It was obvious that Mr Cassidy couldn't move the log on his own. There was still only one way for Mel to get out and that was for Shadow to jump.

Twilight seemed to realize the same

thing. Throwing his head back, he whinnied loudly to Shadow. As he did so, a fork of lightning flashed across the sky, making every hair of his grey body shine with a bright white light.

Suddenly, Lauren saw a new look of bravery flash into Shadow's eyes. Tossing his head back, just like Twilight, he broke into a canter. Mel grabbed hold of his mane with her free hand. Shadow's stride lengthened. His ears pricked and the next second, he was soaring over the burning log, clearing it with ease.

Mel was hanging on to Midnight, a look of astonishment, relief and delight on her face as they galloped up to Twilight. 'He did it!' she said, sliding off

Shadow's back as he halted. 'He jumped it, Lauren! He actually jumped it.'

'He was amazing!' Lauren cried, and

Twilight whinnied in agreement.

Just then Mr Cassidy reached them. 'Mel! Oh my goodness,' he said, his breath coming in short gasps. 'I thought you weren't going to get out. What were you doing in the hay-barn?'

'Rescuing Midnight,' Mel stammered.

'But I told you not to leave the barn,' Mr Cassidy said, pulling her into his arms and kissing her. 'I'm just so glad you're safe.'

'And it's all because of Shadow,' Mel said, breaking free and hugging the dapple-grey pony. 'Wasn't he wonderful, Dad?'

Mr Cassidy smiled at Shadow. 'The best.'

Shadow whickered proudly, happiness lighting up his dark eyes.

As the fire crew arrived and began to put out the fire, Mr Cassidy helped the girls make up a special feed of warm bran, carrots and molasses for Shadow and Twilight. Once the two ponies were dry and bedded down in two stalls, Lauren and Mel went inside.

'I can hardly move I feel so tired,' Mel said, as she and Lauren kicked off their boots by the back door.

'Me too,' Lauren agreed.

Mrs Cassidy was waiting for them. She was upset with Mel for taking such a risk but she was so relieved that both girls were safe that she made them enormous mugs of hot chocolate with marshmallows floating on top.

As Lauren looked out of the kitchen to where the fire crew was saying goodbye to Mr Cassidy, she breathed a sigh of relief. Luckily the flames hadn't spread to the barn, so Mr Cassidy's hay was OK.

In fact, Lauren thought, *everything has turned out OK.* She and Mel and both horses were safe. Midnight, the kitten, had been reunited with Sparkle and Mel had made the little family a new bed in the stall next to Shadow.

Lauren shivered as she realized that it could have all been so different. If it hadn't been for Shadow's bravery, she didn't like to think what might have happened. She remembered the way he had hesitated as he'd approached the log. How had he suddenly found the courage that he needed to jump it?

That night, when Lauren turned Twilight into a unicorn, she asked him if he knew how Shadow had found the courage to jump.

'No, I don't,' Twilight admitted. 'Shall we go and visit him to find out?'

Lauren mounted and, with a kick of Twilight's back legs, they rose into the night sky.

Shadow was grazing near the bottom of his moonlit paddock. Lauren jumped off Twilight's back and ran over to him. 'You were amazing today, Shadow,' she said, as he whinnied a greeting. 'I didn't think you were going to do it but you were so brave. What made you able to jump?'

Shadow neighed.

'He says that when the lightning flashed it made me look like a unicorn,' Twilight translated for Lauren. 'He realized that if he was going to save Mel, he had to be as brave as he was the other night when my horn touched him – as brave as a unicorn.'

Lauren nodded, remembering the look that had come into Shadow's eyes as the lightning had shone on Twilight's coat. It all made sense. She looked at the dapple-grey pony. 'Well, you were wonderful, Shadow, and, best of all, now that you've jumped that great big log, the jumps at Pony Club will seem tiny. You'll be able to jump them easily.'

Shadow snorted doubtfully.

'He doesn't think so,' Twilight interpreted. 'He says that he could only jump the log because he had to.'

Lauren frowned. 'But Twilight wasn't a unicorn when you jumped that log, Shadow. You jumped that log because you were brave.'

Twilight whickered in agreement.

Shadow stared at Lauren as if she'd said something totally astonishing.

'You saved Mel's life, Shadow,' Lauren said softly. 'If you can do that, you can do anything.'

A new look of confidence began to shine in Shadow's eyes.

Lauren climbed on to Twilight's back. 'We'd better go,' she said. 'Goodnight, Shadow.'

Shadow whinnied proudly and tossed his mane as Lauren rode Twilight off into the night.

On Saturday afternoon, Lauren stood beside Twilight, watching Mel ride Shadow towards the first jump in the course that Kathy, their Pony Club trainer, had set out.

It had taken a lot for Lauren to persuade Mel to have a go at the jumping course but, after being reminded of Shadow's huge leap over the burning log, she had finally agreed.

'I don't know why Mel's bothering.' Jade's snide voice cut through the air. She was watching with Monica. 'Shadow's never going to jump a course of jumps – last month he wouldn't even jump one.'

Lauren didn't say anything. She just crossed her fingers. The course was small but twisty and no one in the group had managed a clear round yet.

Jade's pony, Prince, had knocked three fences over and Monica's pony, Scout, had had three refusals. Twilight had only had one fence down, which Lauren didn't mind at all because she knew he'd tried his best. She crossed her fingers as Mel cantered Shadow towards the first jump.

She held her breath. Would Shadow stop?

But, to her delight, the dapple-grey pony's ears pricked up, his stride lengthened and he jumped perfectly over the fence. He cantered to the next one and then the next. As he cleared the last fence, everyone burst into applause for a perfect clear round.

Mel patted Shadow as if she was never going to stop.

Seeing the happiness on Mel's and Shadow's faces, Lauren hugged Twilight in delight. 'Oh, Twilight, isn't it brilliant?' she whispered. 'I'm so glad you were able to help.'

Twilight shook his head and pushed his nose against her chest.

Lauren understood him perfectly. 'OK then,' she said, putting her arm round his neck. 'I'm so glad *we* were able to help!'

My Secret Unicorn

When Lauren recites a secret spell, Twilight turns into a beautiful unicorn with magical powers! Together Lauren and Twilight learn how to use their magic to help their friends.

Look out for more *My Secret Unicorn* adventures:

The Magic spell,
Dreams Come True, Flying High,
Starlight Surprise, Stronger Than Magic,
A Special Friend, A Winter Wish, A Touch of Magic,
Snowy Dreams, Twilight Magic

Have you read them all?

My Secret Unicorn

Flying High

Lauren's friend Jessica doesn't want her father to re-marry. On the day of the wedding, Jessica is so unhappy that she runs away from home. Lauren and Twilight could help Jessica with a little magic, but if they do, will Twilight's secret be safe?

My Secret Unicorn

Starlight Surprise

Lauren doesn't believe in ghosts, but there is definitely something spooky going on down by the creek. Then one night, as Lauren and Twilight fly over the woods near the scary tree house, they make a surprising discovery.

My Secret Unicorn

Stronger Than Magic

Lauren and Twilight have been busy using their special magic to help all their friends, but suddenly Twilight falls ill. Lauren is desperately worried – especially when the vet can find nothing wrong. What can she do to make him well again?

My Secret Unicorn

A Special Friend

Lauren is sure that the little pony
Moonshine is really a unicorn.
But Moonshine has to find a special friend
to make the magic work. Lauren wishes
she and Twilight could help – but what
can they do?

Then Lauren has a brilliant idea . . .

Read more in Puffin

For complete information about books available from Puffin – and Penguin – and how to order them, contact us at the appropriate address below. Please note that for copyright reasons the selection of books varies from country to country.

www.puffin.co.uk

In the United Kingdom: Please write to Dept EP, Penguin Books Ltd, Bath Road, Harmondsworth, West Drayton, Middlesex UB7 ODA

In the United States: Please write to Penguin Group (USA), Inc. P.O. Box 12289, Dept B, Newark, New Jersey 07101–5289 or call 1–800–788–6262

In Canada: Please write to Penguin Books Canada Ltd, 10 Alcorn Avenue, Suite 300, Toronto, Ontario M4V 3B2

In Australia: Please write to Penguin Books Australia Ltd, 250 Camberwell Road, Camberwell, Victoria 3124

In New Zealand: Please write to Penguin Books (NZ) Ltd, Private Bag 102902, North Shore Mail Centre, Auckland 10

In India: Please write to Penguin Books India Pvt Ltd, 11 Panscheel Shopping Centre, Panscheel Park, New Delhi 110 017

In the Netherlands: Please write to Penguin Books Netherlands bv, Postbus 3507, NL–1001 AH Amsterdam

In Germany: Please write to Penguin Books Deutschland GmbH, Metzlerstrasse 26, 60594 Frankfurt am Main

In Spain: Please write to Penguin Books S. A., Bravo Murillo 19, 1° B, 28015 Madrid

In Italy: Please write to Penguin Italia s.r.l., Via Felice Casati 20, I–20124 Milano

In France: Please write to Penguin France S. A., 17 rue Lejeune, F–31000 Toulouse

In Japan: Please write to Penguin Books Japan, Ishikiribashi Building, 2–5–4, Suido, Bunkyo-ku, Tokyo 112

In South Africa: Please write to Longman Penguin Southern Africa (Pty) Ltd, Private Bag X08, Bertsham 2013